# AN OCCASIONALLY HAPPY FAMILY

# AN OCCASIONALLY HAPPY FAMILY

## CLIFF BURKE

HOUGHTON MIFFLIN HARCOURT

BOSTON   NEW YORK

hmhbooks.com

The text was set in Adobe Garamond Pro.
Cover and interior design by Mary Claire Cruz
Interior art by Berat Pekmezci

*Library of Congress Cataloging-in-Publication Data is available.*
ISBN 978-0-358-32567-3

Manufactured in the United States of America
DOC 10 9 8 7 6 5 4 3 2 1

4500822212

*For my grandmother*

*Happy families are all alike; every unhappy family is unhappy in its own way.*

—*Count Leo Nikolayevich Tolstoy*

# ONE

**MY GOAL IN SCHOOL** is to be noticed as little as possible. This is difficult because my school doesn't have walls.

I mean, it has four walls on the outside, but none on the inside. It's one of those "open concept" schools where each grade has its own floor and it's up to the teachers how they want to organize it.

At the beginning of the year, some teachers tried to build their own walls by stacking books floor-to-ceiling around their teaching areas. I liked these enclosed spaces because they were almost like real classrooms. When I was inside them, I didn't have to worry about someone making a face or mouthing a curse word at me from the end of the hallway.

But the walls made of books didn't last very long. It became popular to treat them like giant games of Jenga, and everyone competed to see who could punch out a book without the wall collapsing. When one of the walls finally did collapse and sent two people to the emergency room with broken toes, they were forbidden.

After that, the seventh-grade floor looked like a small, messy bus station with chairs arranged in little clusters every ten feet or so. The teachers would wheel stained whiteboards in front of their assigned chair clusters and try to shout over the commotion. The sounds from one class bled into the sounds from the next so that there was a consistent hum of noise just distracting enough to never hear anything that your teacher was trying to yell in your class's direction.

I learned to deal with the constant noise and peering eyes by focusing my attention on my notebook. While the teacher shouted and the rest of the class talked, I drew. Sometimes doodles—the classic spirals and sketches of teachers saying things like "Hello, I'm stupid"—but mostly cool stuff like aliens and robots.

Last year, in sixth grade, I started working on my first graphic novel trilogy. Part one, *The Aliens Who Ate People and Never Got Full*, debuted at my lunch table on the last day of the school year and was a big hit with my three friends—Liam, Angel P., and Rajneesh. I spent all year working on the sequel, *The Humans Who Fought Back by Eating the Aliens Who Ate People*, and promised that it would be ready to read on the last day of school. Now that the big day had come, I rushed to finish the final page before lunch.

I drew the main character, Laurence Stronghouse, lifting the last living alien to his mouth. "Bon appétit," he says, biting into the alien's skull and releasing a green goo that spells out *The End*. As I went over the word bubble with a darker pen, the bell rang. The entire class leaped up and sprinted toward the cafeteria. I waited for the ink to dry, closed my notebook, and joined the herd.

Rajneesh and Angel P. were already eating when I sat down at our usual table.

"Today's the day," Rajneesh said.

"I hope it doesn't suck," Angel P. added.

"It doesn't suck," I said nervously, hoping that it didn't.

"We'll be the judge of that," Liam announced, awkwardly slamming his lunch tray onto the table like a gavel.

I took out my notebook and slid it their way. I watched their faces as they flipped through the pages, trying to gauge whether or not I'd satisfied my three fans. There were a lot of smiles, but not as many laughs as I would have liked.

"Wellll?" I finally asked.

"It rules," Angel P. said.

"It's even better than the first one," Rajneesh agreed.

"It's good," Liam said hesitantly, "but could I offer some critical colleagues?"

"Critical colleagues" is what our school calls criticism. Whenever we write a paper or finish a project, we have to sit in a circle and offer critical feedback for our "colleagues." Most people smile and say nice things while the teacher is watching. Then as soon as the teacher turns around they offer feedback like "You think you're better than me, huh?" while ripping your paper in half.

"We don't need critical colleagues," Angel P. said. "It's awesome. Seriously."

"Yeah, shut up, Liam," Rajneesh said.

"You shut up," Liam said.

"Both of you shut up," I said. "What's wrong with it?"

Liam was my least favorite of my three friends and someone I never hung out with one-on-one, but I still respected his opinion. Even if it was usually misguided.

"Nothing's *wrong* with it," Liam said. "I just don't see where you can go from here. In the first book, the aliens eat people. In the second book, the people eat aliens. What's going to happen in the third book? There's no one left to eat."

"There's not going to be a third book," I said.

"But didn't you say this was going to be a trilogy?" Liam said.

I did say that two years ago, but realized pretty early in the sequel that, as Liam pointed out, there was nowhere left to go. Instead, I told them, I had begun plotting the idea for a new, more realistic series called *Bob: The Boy with Perfect Memory*, which would tell the story of a boy who remembered every second from every day of his life.

"That. Sounds. Incredible," Rajneesh said.

"So sick," Angel P. said.

Liam contorted his face into an expression that meant he didn't like it.

"You have a problem with this, too?" I said.

"Not a problem," Liam said. "I just don't understand how that's a story. Someone remembers everything. So what? What's the conflict?"

"Well," I said, "since he remembers everything, he has trouble, you know, getting over things."

"Like what?" Liam asked.

"Like big things that happen to him."

"Can you give an example?"

"Like when his mom dies," I mumbled.

They all looked down at the table. Liam started fidgeting with his milk carton, clearly unsure what to say next. It wasn't exactly the reaction I was hoping for.

"Well, that's certainly . . . a . . . conflict," Liam muttered while still staring at the lip of his milk.

"It's just an early idea," I said quickly. "A rough draft. We'll see how it goes."

I took a bite of my peanut butter sandwich and waited for someone else to speak.

After several excruciating seconds of silence, Angel P. finally asked Rajneesh, "So when does Robot Camp start?"

"It's not Robot Camp," Rajneesh said. "It's *Robotics* Camp and it starts next Monday. There are still two spots left if—"

"I'm busy," Angel P. said. "Camp *Earth Death* starts as soon as I get home."

*Earth Death* was a new online multiplayer game where you tried to gather as many resources as possible to prepare for the death of the earth. The easiest way to gather resources was by killing people and taking all their stuff. Angel P. was very good at killing people and taking their stuff. So good that he never "risked" letting me play with him.

"There's a camp for that?" Rajneesh asked.

"I'm gonna camp out in my room and play every day," Angel P. said.

"Well, I'm going to *Florida* for a few weeks," Liam said.

"No one cares," Angel P. said.

"I care," Liam said.

"I'm going somewhere too," I said.

"Like, somewhere cool?" Angel P. asked.

"I don't know," I said. "My dad said he'd tell me after school."

"It's probably not as cool as Florida," Liam grumbled.

"We're not sitting together next year," Angel P. said to Liam as the bell rang.

**DAD IS A HIGH SCHOOL** science teacher who looks and acts like a high school science teacher. Because the high school is next to the middle school and ends around the same time, he always drives me home. On days when there wasn't a Journalism, Yearbook, or Drama Club meeting, my older sister, Laura, was also along for the ride. She was less than a year away from her sixteenth birthday and kept a running countdown to the day when she could drive herself.

Usually, I opened the car door to Laura complaining and Dad waiting for her to stop. But when I stepped into the car today, Laura squealed, "Theo's here! Now you can tell me!"

"Tell you what?" I asked.

"Where we're going, duh," she said.

Dad was big on traditions and had made it our family tradition to leave for a one-week vacation every first of July. In order, our last four vacations were to Grandma's house in Oklahoma, Grandma's house in Oklahoma, Disney World, and Grandma's house in Oklahoma. But over the past few weeks, he'd hinted at a vacation destination that didn't involve Oklahoma or our grandmother. He even seemed to be doing some advance planning and kept going outside to make mysterious, secretive phone calls.

"Be patient," Dad said as he started the car. "All things come to those who are patient."

"That's not how that quote goes," Laura said.

"I wasn't quoting anything," Dad said.

"You were trying to," Laura said. "But you said it wrong. It's 'all things come to those who wait.'"

"That's one way to say it," Dad said.

"It's the correct way to say it," Laura said.

"Hey, I was just wondering," I said. "Where are we going?"

"I'll tell you in a minute," Dad said. "Just . . . be . . . patient."

"Are you trying to quote again?" I asked.

"I'm just trying to put my own words together," Dad said.

"You're not doing a very good job," I said.

"I have a quote," Laura said. "Where are we going?"

"Who said that?" Dad asked.

"Theo did, a minute ago."

Dad looked sharply in the rearview mirror. After inspecting our faces, he resignedly said, "Fine, I'll tell you."

Laura and I cheered from the back seat.

"Drumroll, please," Dad said.

"No," Laura said.

I lightly tapped on my knees while Dad thunderously pounded the sides of the steering wheel.

He put on his game-show-announcer voice and said, "We're . . . going . . . toooo . . . *Big Bend National Parrrrrkkkkkk!*"

Laura and I stared confusedly at his reflection in the rearview mirror.

"Wait, what?" Laura said.

"Is that . . . good?" I asked. As a native Texan, I had heard of Big Bend National Park but didn't know anything about it. I pictured a flexible person camping.

"Yes, I think it's *very* good," Dad said.

Laura took out her phone and immediately scrolled through a hundred pictures of Big Bend. "It looks pretty nice, I guess," she said.

"It's more than nice," Dad said. As he kept talking about how good his idea was, I took out my phone and conducted my own research.

"And the best thing about it," Dad continued, "it's totally free."

"I don't think that's true," Laura said.

"I'm telling you, it is. Craig and I went back in ninety-four and we didn't spend a single dollar the whole weekend. You can ask him. He'll tell you the same thing."

Craig is Dad's only friend and his truth-telling abilities are questionable.

"I'm not going to ask him," Laura said, still scrolling through Big Bend pictures. "I can see this being kind of okay, though."

"See, you're coming around," Dad said.

I was less enthused. Different websites described the experience of spending July in Big Bend as "uncomfortably hot," "deeply unpleasant," and "hell on earth."

"What do you think, Theo?" Dad asked me.

I didn't want to spoil his good mood. He had clearly tried to find a fun family vacation for us. Unfortunately, his idea of fun involved camping in the desert in Texas in July, but at least he was trying.

"It's better than Grandma's house in Oklahoma," I said.

# THREE

**FOR THE NEXT THREE WEEKS,** Dad told everyone who'd listen (me; grocery store employees; his only friend, Craig) about our free vacation. "Can you believe that a family can still pack up the car and go on vacation for *free?*" he said repeatedly. It seemed unlikely, but since I wouldn't be paying for anything anyways, I wasn't that concerned.

I was more worried about the planning side of things. Our last four vacations didn't require much preparation. A call to Grandma covered most of them, and Disney World, from what Dad said, just asked you to pick the price you were willing to pay. (He must have picked one of the lowest prices, because we stayed in a hotel twenty miles away.)

Luckily, Laura was far more proactive. After Dad announced his plan, she spent the next week on our shared computer creating a workable daily itinerary.

In her research, Laura also discovered that visiting a national park does, in fact, cost money. She kept quiet about it for a while, but two weeks before our planned July 1 departure, she confronted Dad at breakfast. As he and I sat leisurely enjoying our meal, Laura purposefully strode into the kitchen carrying a large notebook, took her usual seat, and asked directly, "Dad, have you done *any* research?"

"No 'good morning'?" he said.

"Good morning," Laura said dismissively. "Have you done any research about our upcoming vacation?"

"Um," he said, considering, "a little. Probably more than you think. But mostly, uh, no."

"Dad."

"We still have two weeks."

"Dad," she repeated.

He put his hand over his heart. "I promise I will dedicate one full day to research before we leave."

"I've already dedicated several days," Laura said.

"When?"

"When you were watching TV. When you were pretending to meditate. When you were sitting here, eating breakfast, choosing not to plan your family vacation for your family."

"I've been busy," he tried to explain. "And I'm not pretending to meditate. But I can start researching tomorrow if that'd make you feel better."

"Uh-huh, sure. But I *have* researched, so . . ."

Laura paused to allow Dad to ask a follow-up question. He picked up his spoon and continued to eat cereal.

"Would you like to hear what I've found out?" she said, exasperated.

"Yes, yes, of course. I was just about to ask you," he said. "And I do appreciate it, the work you've done. I don't mean to not recognize the effort that you've put in."

"It's fine, calm down," Laura said, opening her notebook, labeled *Big Bend,* to the first page, titled *General Notes.* "So, first — everything you said about how the park is free and won't it be such a joy to 'experience nature without a price tag'? Do you remember saying that phrase?"

Dad sighed.

"Well, turns out you're wrong. Big Bend costs twenty-five dollars. Per car. Per week. If we stay even one hour over the one-week limit? We have to pay for another week." She flipped to the next page. "There are also multiple sleeping options, but most people decide to either camp or stay in the lodges. Both of those options? Cost money."

"Is this from a trusted website?" Dad asked.

"The dot gov website, which, again, you could have spent three minutes reading, but I'm not trying to criticize."

"I believe you," he said. "It's just that it *was* free when Craig and I went."

"You've said that," Laura remarked. "But it's definitely *not* free now. Also, all the reviews say the campgrounds are disgusting in July and we should definitely pay to stay in the lodges instead."

"Disgusting how?" he asked.

Laura flipped ahead in her notes. "This person said, 'Under no circumstances will I ever camp here again. There were no showers, an active hornet's nest in the one available bathroom, and the water tasted like boiled spit.'"

"That's just one review," he said. "I'm sure other people have had better experiences."

"Here's another one," Laura said, turning to the next page. "'While my family has loved camping here in February, I will never again spend the summer in Big Bend. After three days in one-hundred-ten-degree weather, I wanted to end my life.'"

"So maybe camping will be a little . . . *difficult,*" Dad said. "But we can't spend the whole time in a lodge."

"Yes, we can," Laura said.

"I wouldn't mind spending the whole time in a lodge," I added.

"It wouldn't be the whole time anyways," Laura said. "It'd just be at night. Where we could shower. Instead of using a hornet-infested bathroom."

Dad sighed. "How much are the lodges?"

"One hundred dollars," Laura said quietly.

*"One hundred dollars?"*

"Per night," Laura added. "I told you it wasn't free."

"I'm willing to pitch in five dollars," I suggested.

Dad paused for a moment to think, gazing intently into his cereal bowl.

"I have five more reviews of the campgrounds here, all bad," Laura said, sliding her notebook in Dad's direction.

He picked it up and slowly read through two pages of one-star reviews before closing the notebook and setting it aside.

"Here's what we can do," he said. "I'll pay for three nights at the lodge, but we need to camp at least one night. I'm not going all the way to Big Bend to not camp at least once. And I already asked Craig if I could borrow his tent."

"But what about the other two nights?" Laura asked. "Aren't we going for a week?"

Dad smiled. "I've got a little surprise for the other two nights."

"Wait, what? What surprise?" Laura asked.

"If I told you, it wouldn't be a surprise."

"Then how about it's not a surprise and you tell me instead."

"It's better as a surprise."

"Can you tell *me?*" I asked.

"No," Dad said, collecting our cereal bowls and walking toward the sink. "It's a surprise for both of you."

Laura and I eyed each other uncertainly.

"Can we guess what it is?" I asked.

"No," Dad said.

"Why not?" I asked.

"It's not the right time," Dad said.

"Then when *can* we guess?" Laura asked.

"At the right time," Dad said.

"Which is when?" Laura asked.

"Not right now," Dad said.

"Will you tell us when it *is* the right time?" Laura asked.

"I'll let you know," he said before walking out of the kitchen.

# FOUR

**THE MORNING WE LEFT,** I had to drop our cat, Larry, off at our next-door neighbor's house. He was only five years old but had already settled into old age. Since turning three, he'd pared his daily schedule down to one hour of eating and twenty-three hours of sleeping. I tried to convince Dad that bringing along a sleeping cat wouldn't be much trouble, and even did some research to prove my point, but the phrase "discreet portable litter box" quickly ended the discussion.

So instead of loading a peacefully resting cat into our car, I had to wake Larry up, lure him into a cage, and carry him next door. He'd already fallen back asleep before I rang the doorbell.

"Theo. It's so good to see you," Mrs. Stilden said, opening her door with an inviting smile. "Your dad said you had something for us?"

I lifted the cage and she peered at Larry's rising and falling chest.

"He won't be much trouble, I promise," I said. "He won't ask to be pet or scratched or played with or anything. You just have to feed him."

"I think I can handle that. Bring him on in," she said, waving for me to follow.

Mrs. and Mr. Stilden are both retired professors and used to watch Laura and me after school. It had been a while since I'd been over but nothing had changed. Half the house was covered with books, expensive-looking paintings, and pictures of their family in golden frames. The other half of the house, the basement, was dedicated to Mr. Stilden's model train workshop. Mrs. Stilden could be a little nosy but had always given me a quiet space to draw whenever I wanted. Mr. Stilden communicated in hour-long monologues about trains and put me to work painting miniature lighthouses if I ever stepped foot downstairs.

"You know," she said, leading me into the living room, "I was going through my photo albums the other day and found a picture that I think you might like."

My entire body tensed. As I sat down on the couch, she passed me a picture of my family from five years ago. "That was the day y'all moved in next door. Do you remember?"

In the picture, Laura and I look like little kids. We're side by side, hanging on to cleanly painted black railings on the front porch. Behind us, Dad's holding up the new key like a golden ticket while Mom's posed with her hands on the doorknob, ready to dramatically open the front door. On all our faces are bright, goofy smiles.

I held the picture for a few seconds without saying anything. That familiar feeling rose through my body, and before I could stop them, tears started running down my cheeks. I leaned my head back and took a few deep breaths.

"I'm sorry, honey," Mrs. Stilden said. "I didn't mean to upset you. I thought it was a nice picture. But I can see that—"

"No, no, it's okay," I said, sniffling. I don't usually start crying at the sight of my mom, but this had caught me off-guard. I'd gotten used to the one remaining picture of her that Dad had kept up in our house. But this was a new picture, one that hadn't become wallpaper.

Mrs. Stilden joined me on the couch, politely offering a box of tissues. "I miss her too, you know. We all do," she said while waiting for me to dry my eyes.

"I didn't mean to get so emotional," I said apologetically as I wiped away my tears. "It *is* a nice picture. Would you actually mind if I, um, kept it?"

"Of course, darling." She gave my hand a comforting squeeze as I carefully slipped the picture into my pocket. "I have more pictures, you know. But we don't have to get into them right now. Why don't you tell me how you've been? You're still drawing, I hope?"

"Yes," I said, happy to change subjects.

"Still drawing those aliens?" she asked.

"My work has matured," I said, not wanting to get into *Bob: The Boy with Perfect Memory* in detail. "I'm trying to do more realistic stories now."

"That sounds like a nice change. And how about your sister? Your father?"

"Laura's the same. She planned this whole trip for us, more or less. Dad's been really busy this year, I think. That's what he's told us. He's been going on a lot of hikes and trying to meditate and stuff. But, you know, good."

"I'm happy to hear it. Sounds like you're all doing well," she said.

"I guess," I said. I didn't exactly think we were "doing well," but I didn't want to talk about how I really felt and risk crying again.

In the brief quiet that followed, she opened Larry's cage and dragged him onto her lap. "You're sure he's . . . alive?" she asked, lifting one of Larry's legs and watching it fall lifelessly back down.

"Pretty sure," I said.

"Well," she said, "I'm sure y'all want to get going soon. Give all my love to Laura and your father. I'm happy that he's going out and doing things again. You know, these past few years *have* been challenging for him. I hope you and Laura both know that. I'd give you a hug but I don't want to disrupt Larry's nap." She blew me a kiss instead. "Promise me that you'll have fun on your trip."

"I promise I'll have fun on my trip," I said unenthusiastically.

# FIVE

**DAD AND LAURA** were already packing up the car when I returned. She'd carefully considered, written, and printed out a checklist last week, but this was the first time Dad had read it all the way through.

"Why does it say 'whatever gross snacks Dad bought'?" he asked.

"Because you buy gross snacks," she said.

"You think vegetable-flavored potato sticks are gross?"

"Did you seriously pack those?"

"You'll like them, trust me."

"I won't, trust me," Laura said. "Go to the next line."

"'Amazing snacks Laura bought,'" he read.

"Check."

"Cooler?"

"Next to your foot."

"You tried Craig's tent yesterday? Everything's in working order?"

"Check and check."

"And your brother?"

"Is behind you."

"Larry's gone," I said. "Now he won't bother you by silently sleeping in the back seat."

"Larry will be much happier with the Stildens. We all agreed on this," Dad said.

"I disagreed, but am powerless," I said.

"You're not powerless, but Larry is. Thank you for taking him next door. Is there anything else that either of you need?" he asked.

"No," Laura said, scanning the checklist and making sure each box was thoroughly checked. "I have everything."

"I'm good," I said, having packed my suitcase with all the clean clothes in my drawers.

"You both went to the bathroom?" Dad asked.

"Ew. Yes," Laura said as she finished hauling the cooler into the back of our old SUV.

"I could go," I said, taking my last opportunity to enjoy some alone time before being stuck in a car and then lodge and then tent with my family for a week.

I was a little worried about how we'd survive in such close quarters. We'd never been on a vacation with just the three of us for a full week. When we went to Grandma's, Dad mostly hung around the house while Grandma drove Laura and me around. We came together as a whole family only for dinner.

The vacation to Disney World was the last time Laura, Dad, Mom, and I had traveled together. Two months after we got back, Mom died. Or "passed away," as everyone else says. It wasn't sudden like maybe it sounds. She had cancer and knew she was going to die for a full year before she did. Those twelve months were a sort of countdown, a chance to "appreciate every day" or however you wanted to look at it.

During that time, Mom and Dad's room was turned into a mini hospital room, and she spent most of the day in bed on heavy medication. Laura and I were kept busy mornings and afternoons—going to school, directly to the Stildens' after, and back to our house for dinner at seven—but we were both given an hour a day when we could go into the room to sit and talk to Mom.

She wasn't the same person I knew from the first ten years of my life. The medicine made her loopy, and she either told us stories or described her dreams. But it was what I got toward the end, so I looked forward to that hour after dinner when I'd get to go into her room.

I can barely remember anything she said now, but it's still the clearest memory I have of her: in bed, smiling, laying out her arms on both sides as an invitation for me and Laura to come snuggle. That was what I saw now as I walked past Dad's room, formerly their room, on my last lap through the house.

I don't usually spend a lot of time thinking about Mom except for moments like this, when I know that I'm about to do something new and she won't be there to see it. Or even to hear about it later.

Mrs. Stilden was right that maybe I hadn't thought enough about how Dad was feeling, but he hadn't wanted to talk about things with me either—not since the funeral and the week after. It wasn't like I hadn't considered how difficult it must've been to suddenly become a single parent. But if he didn't want to talk about it, I wasn't going to ask him. We'd all been in recovery mode for the past two years, living our lives the same way we did during the year when Mom was sick, just without her in the house anymore.

Maybe this trip was Dad's way of getting us excited about spending time together without her. Maybe that was also why this was more of an idea than an actual plan. But Laura had taken that original thought and turned it into a series of daily itineraries that wouldn't leave us stranded in the wilderness.

I made sure the front door was locked and joined my family in the car.

# SIX

**THE CAR RIDE** from our house in Austin to Grandma's in Oklahoma City usually takes six hours. Although the ride to Big Bend would take eight hours, Dad's Family Road Trip Rules remained the same.

1. We could each use our phone for up to two hours. (This was easy to get around. If you used your phone for twenty minutes every hour, Dad didn't have the attention level or mental awareness to add up the fact that you'd actually gone over the limit. The only way to get caught was to use your phone for three hours continuously.)

2. We could each sleep for one hour, but not at the same time. (He claimed that if he looked in the rearview mirror and saw us both sleeping, he'd fall asleep too.)

3. We could not criticize his driving. (He never went more than two miles per hour over the speed limit and was frequently passed, honked at, and given the middle finger. In all instances, he responded by smiling and waving.)

4. He controlled the music. (He enjoys dumb and bad music. His favorite band is the Grateful Dead, and he loves to "boogie" in his seat to their twenty-eight-minute-long songs about walking down the street or whatever.)

For the first hour, Dad talked. It started as a conversation between the two of us but soon devolved into an uninterrupted monologue. Among other topics, he explained how sunsets were beautiful, sunscreen was underrated, and mosquitoes were bad. Laura had earbuds in, using her first phone hour to ignore him. I said "uh-huh" every other minute while looking out the window.

While he described how his "sweet blood" was "catnip" for mosquitoes, the sun broke through the clouds and the car became incredibly hot. Dad periodically made minor adjustments to the temperature, alternating between rolling the windows down and moving the air conditioning from low to high to off. Whatever adjustments he made, it remained incredibly hot.

After two hours, Laura took out her earbuds.

"That's two hours," Dad said.

"I'm fully aware," Laura said, stretching out and preparing to transition into her sleeping hour.

"Theo and I are having a pretty good conversation," Dad said. "You're missing out."

I had said maybe seven words since the start of our trip.

"I'm good," Laura said, shutting her eyes.

"I have another idea, then," Dad said, unrelenting. "Theo, do you see that paper on the front seat?" I leaned forward and grabbed a folded piece of computer paper. It was a printed-out article titled "50 Fun Questions to Get Your Kids Talking" from GoodParents.com.

I snorted. "Good parents dot com?"

"It's a good website," Dad said.

"What is this?" Laura asked, leaping to life and snatching the paper out of my hands. "Oh my god, Dad," she said, scanning the list. "You know you're not supposed to print this out. You're supposed to, like, read it and remember the questions."

"There were too many questions to remember," Dad said.

"These are so stupid," Laura said.

"I thought they were all right," Dad said. "They have us talking, as promised."

"Question number one," Laura read. "What do you like daydreaming about? Well, Dad?"

"They're supposed to be questions for you," Dad said.

"I'm being the good parent right now," Laura said. "Tell me: What do you like daydreaming about?"

He paused thoughtfully. "I like daydreaming about my two lovely children growing up to be responsible, respectable adults," he said in total cheese mode.

We groaned for one full minute.

I grabbed the list from Laura and read, "Number four: If you could do anything right now, what would you do?"

"I'll answer this one," Laura jumped in. "If I could do anything right now, I'd be sleeping in my room with the door closed and the air conditioning on full blast."

"I'd also be at home," I said. "Air conditioning fully blasting. Laura would be gone. And I'd be drawing."

"If *I* could do anything right now," Dad said, "I'd be right where I am — in the car, traveling toward one of the great natural wonders of our state, ready to surprise my wonderful children with a trip they'll never forget."

We groaned for two full minutes.

"Can I ask a question that's *not* on the list?" Laura said.

"I don't see why not," Dad said.

"Can you tell us what the surprise is now?" Laura asked.

"It's still too early," Dad said. "A surprise is supposed to be like I show you something and then go 'SURPRISE!' and you're, you know, surprised. I can't tell you in advance."

"So you're going to show us something?" Laura said.

"That was just an example," Dad said.

"But it is a *thing?*" I asked. "You're going to *give* us something?"

"I know it's not a thing," Laura said. "Because you said the surprise was for two nights. That means it's a place."

"I'll say nothing more about the surprise," Dad said.

"I'm right that it's a place, though?" Lara asked.

"My lips are sealed," he said. "Now pass me the list and we'll do this properly. A good parent asking his good children some good questions."

I handed him the paper. He skimmed through the list while slipping below the speed limit. A truck driver sped past with middle finger raised. "Number sixteen: If your stuffed animals could talk, what would they say?"

"I'm going to sleep," Laura said.

"I'm kidding," Dad said. "Here's a good one. Number thirty-nine: What's your superhero name and what would your superpowers be?"

"That's easy," Laura said. "I'd be One-Year-Older Woman. A sixteen-year-old woman who can drive. My superpower would be driving myself on our family vacations while you and Theo follow behind asking each other good parents dot com questions."

"I'd be Only-Child Man," I said. "My superpower would be living my life without Laura."

"Those aren't very nice," Dad said.

"Who said they have to be nice?" I said.

"Well, I have a nice one," Dad said. "If I could be any super-hero, I'd be Super-Dad. And my superpower would be doing everything I can to love and support my children."

We never stopped groaning.

# SEVEN

**AT HOUR FOUR,** I tried to sleep but couldn't. I also couldn't read or draw in a moving car. I've tried, many times, and always ended up with a headache.

Two weeks earlier, I'd started working on *Bob: The Boy with Perfect Memory* and had already finished the first few pages. The beginning shows how Bob uses his memory to his advantage. He learns to speak French, Spanish, and Chinese. Despite being only twelve, he takes and aces the SAT and gets into college for free. He wins the *Jeopardy!* Teen Tournament for one full month until he's forced to step aside. They let him go on real *Jeopardy!* and he wins $4 million before deciding that beating everyone isn't fun anymore.

Because of all this, Bob becomes a minor celebrity. In a live interview, a reporter asks him if his perfect memory has any downsides. As he pauses to think, I show Bob's mind flashing to the day that his mother died. He can remember every minute and every feeling from that day. His eyes start to well up. "Yes," Bob says. "There are some things I wish I could forget."

The next panel shows a scientist in Switzerland watching the interview on a big screen. The scientist becomes intrigued by Bob's condition and starts working on a pill that would alter his perfect memory, allowing Bob to live like a "normal" person.

I hadn't decided whether Bob was going to take the pill, and the decision would have to wait until we arrived at the park and I had more time to draw.

Because I wanted to save my phone hours for later, there was only one thing left to do: aimlessly stare out the window. I leaned back and fixed my gaze outside. Unfortunately, there wasn't much to see. At least from the highway, Texas cannot be described as a feast for the eyes. There were gas stations, and there were cows, and there was grass. The gas stations looked empty, the cows looked miserable, and the grass looked dead.

When we traveled to Disney World, it was much easier. We were on an airplane with little TVs in the seats. It wasn't uncomfortably hot. We could go to the bathroom without "killing momentum" (Dad's words). And there were still four of us.

Everyone was in bright spirits when we boarded the airplane. It was ten months after the doctors told Mom she had terminal cancer, and it seemed like she might live longer than expected. We didn't know that it was only two months before she would die.

At the time I didn't think of it as our last trip as a whole family. I must have known on some level, but I didn't put the pieces together that it was a significant, final family vacation. I was eleven and just happy to go to Disney World. I even got upset sometimes when Mom had to go back to the hotel after a few hours and we didn't get to go on all the rides, which I feel terrible about now.

Laura, however, was fully aware that it was our last family trip and went out of her way to make sure everyone was having a good time. For the entire week, she stopped acting like her usual bossy and disagreeable self. When Mom said she needed a break, Laura offered to take the shuttle back to the hotel with her. If Mom didn't feel like going to the park at all, Laura stayed behind and watched TV with her. She thought that if Mom could see how helpful she was, how much fun the two of them could have together, maybe she'd live a little longer.

I didn't know this was Laura's plan until the day after Mom died, when Laura came rushing into my room late at night to ask me what else she could have done. Did I think that if she wasn't in so many after-school clubs—if Mom hadn't had to drive her to and from school every day, and take her to ballet on Saturdays—Mom might have lived longer? Did I think that all the times she cried in Mom's bedroom during the last year of her life made Mom too sad to keep living? That maybe she was tired of watching her daughter come into her room and cry every night?

I'd never thought about it like that—that anything I did could have an effect on Mom's health. The day Dad said she had terminal cancer and told me what "terminal" meant, I understood that she'd be gone soon. When he said that she had one year to live, I believed it. I *hoped* it wasn't true, but deep down I knew that it was and that there was nothing I could do about it. It's not that I wasn't sad; I just never thought I was involved in the process, and so I never took any responsibility for what happened. I didn't say any of this to Laura, though. Instead, I told her what Dad said the afternoon Mom died: It wasn't Laura's fault. It wasn't anybody's fault. Dying just happens.

But Laura wasn't convinced. She thought there were reasons behind everything, and over the last two years had become obsessed with researching why and how things happen. It started with cancer. She spent the weeks after Mom died reading every link at the bottom of the cancer Wikipedia entry. Even the really complicated ones that looked like they were written for doctors. Eventually, she'd collected enough data to understand how cancer spreads through the body and accepted that driving someone to ballet practice does not increase the harm of cancer cells; it's just an activity you can take part in while cancer cells continue to break down your body.

Dad said her research was "healthy," and allowed her to hog our shared computer to finish her report. I say "report" because that's what she was doing—not just looking up information but organizing it into a paper called "Laura's Brief: A Better Understanding of Cancer."

The research didn't end there. "Laura's Brief: America's Dangerous Obsession with Sports" and "Laura's Brief: How Gender Inequality Starts in Schools" soon followed. After finalizing our travel plans and itinerary, Laura investigated the history of the United States National Park Service. Before we left, she printed out "Laura's Brief: The True History of Big Bend National Park."

Dad wasn't as excited about this report but didn't let Laura know. I knew his true feelings when I saw him pick it up earlier that morning, read through a few paragraphs, roll his eyes, and set it back down with a sigh.

# EIGHT

**AS WE WAITED** in the line of cars at the entrance to Big Bend, Dad made his first mention of Laura's latest brief.

With a slight smile, he asked, "Are you going to share your *brief* with the park ranger?"

Laura wasn't amused. "Is that a real question or are you making fun of me?"

"It's a real question," he said. "Do you want to share your Wikipedia research about the National Park Service with the park ranger?"

"So you're making fun of me."

"Just teasing."

"It's not nice. And I didn't just use Wikipedia. I read the National Park Service's website and it said, 'The park was established in 1933, when boundary unrest in the area ended.' I didn't know what that meant, so I had to look up what *boundary unrest* was going on in the area."

"We'll see what the ranger has to say about *boundary unrest*," Dad said, pulling up to the front of the line and rolling down his window.

The park ranger, in his full tan uniform and hat, sat in a small office behind glass. "What can I do for you?" he asked through a microphone without looking up.

"Good evening," Dad said. "We have one vehicle. Three people."

"That'll be thirty dollars."

"Thirty?" Dad was, as always, ready to argue about an increased price. "The website said twenty-five dollars per car. Laura, back me up here."

Laura rolled down her window and leaned forward to make eye contact with the ranger. "It does say twenty-five dollars online."

The park ranger looked at Laura and spoke matter-of-factly, like he'd repeated this exact statement all day. "It is ordinarily twenty-five dollars per vehicle, yes. But today being July first, and Thursday being July fourth, that makes this a holiday week. And on a holiday week, there is an additional five-dollar charge. The website also expresses this."

Dad started to say something but Laura interrupted. "But why does it cost more for a holiday? Shouldn't it cost less? Don't you *want* people to celebrate the Fourth of July here?"

"I don't create the pricing guidelines, young lady. I just enforce them."

"Don't call me young lady. I'm not questioning the pricing guidelines. I'm genuinely curious. Why do *you* think it costs more?"

"Well, if you really want my opinion, young lady—"

"Please stop saying young lady."

"Okay, well, uh, ma'am."

"Ma'am is worse. My name is Laura. You can say Laura if you feel like you need to."

"All right, then . . . Laura. I'd be happy to answer your question." He straightened up in his chair, honored to be asked about his opinion. "We have a saying here that the national parks are one of America's greatest democratic ideas. That this land belongs to all people and is protected for them to visit whenever they'd like. A small increase in price for public holidays helps us to keep this park open and protected. Personally, I think there's no better way to celebrate America's birthday than by contributing a few extra dollars toward our cause."

"A wonderful sentiment," Dad said. "We understand the small price increase and are happy to pay."

But Laura wasn't satisfied. "That all sounds good, but do you know the *true* history of this park?"

"Of course I do. I've worked here for seventeen years. I've been in this booth every morning since before you were born."

"Then you know that it's stolen land?" Laura said. "Land that used to belong to the Comanches. And to Mexico. That United States soldiers killed Native Americans and Mexicans to *protect* this land that was never theirs in the first place. That it only became a 'national park' when some rich white farmer decided to sell it to the government because he was tired of looking after it himself."

"That's not exactly what happened."

"That's my general understanding. I've done a lot of reading. Probably more than you have."

The park ranger took off his hat and leaned so close to the microphone that his face nearly squished against the glass. "Look, young lady. You and your dad, and that other little kid back there, drove to this park. If you don't want to be here, you can turn around and leave. My job is to sell tickets to the people who want to *enjoy* the natural wonders of the United States. A country I'm proud to be a part of. What I am *not* paid to do is listen to some teenager spout conspiracy theories about the history of this here park. Which was not stolen. It was *fought for* and *earned*."

Laura wasn't going to back down. I could see in her face that she was ready to release the full factual fury of "Laura's Brief: The True History of Big Bend National Park," but Dad reached back and put his hand over her mouth.

"A fine speech, Mr., uh, Ranger," he said, struggling to open his wallet with one hand while still muzzling Laura. "We love and appreciate your work and will gladly pay the thirty dollars if you will take it by card."

Laura, still struggling, let out a muffled shriek before flinging herself backwards into her seat and angrily lodging earbuds into both ears.

"A card will be just fine," the park ranger said, leaning away from the window and adjusting his uniform. "I sincerely do hope you all enjoy your stay. Here's a pamphlet with the real, complete history of the park for the young lady in the back."

He handed Dad a ticket to stick to the windshield and three thick Big Bend National Park booklets and clicked the gate open. As it swung up, Dad apologized and thanked him.

Laura, window still down, moved out of sight of the rearview mirror and gave the finger to the ranger as we rolled by. In solidarity with Laura, I gave him the finger, too.

# NINE

**WE HADN'T EATEN** a full meal since leaving at noon, so the first thing Dad wanted to do was drive directly to our lodge for dinner. The GPS had it at thirty-five minutes away and we spent the duration in silence. Dad never turned the music back on. Laura never took her earbuds out.

This had been happening a lot lately. He and Laura would get into some argument that I had nothing to do with, and he'd act like he was mad at me, too. It was then my job to get everyone talking again, and I was tired of it. Laura created her own messes and would have to start dealing with them. And if Dad was so mad at her, he would have to start dealing with it directly instead of just waiting it out. Rather than intervening, I returned to my old pastime: aimlessly gazing out the window.

It was beautiful, if your idea of beauty is lumpy hills of dirt covered with rocks. The majesty of rocky brown lumps bloomed in every direction. It did look more like a Star Wars planet than most of Texas, which to some people is, I guess, interesting.

I flipped through the official Big Bend booklet to see how the experts described it: "weather-beaten," "profoundly isolated," "never-ending." I also felt weather-beaten and profoundly isolated after the full day of car travel, so I could relate.

It's not that I hate nature. I like green grass and trees and mountains just fine. I even liked most of the pictures of Big Bend I'd seen, but this part of the park wasn't prominently featured online. I tried to roll down my window to see if the air smelled cleaner, as the booklet claimed, but Dad had the locks on. I sighed and continued silently staring at withered dirt formations.

When we pulled into the Chisos Mountains Lodge parking lot, the sun was setting and Dad's mood was restored. He didn't consider my mood (not great) or Laura's mood (very bad) and instead leaped out of the car and started walking around in amazement.

I joined him, eager to stretch my legs, but Laura stayed in the car.

"Big. Bend. National. Park," he said, coming over to put his hand on my shoulder. "Would you look at that *sunset*."

It looked like a normal sunset to me. "It's, uh, something," I said.

"Something very special."

I struggled to find more to say. After a few seconds I said, "It kind of looks like a desktop background."

"Not everything is like a computer," Dad said. He kept staring ahead while taking deeper than necessary breaths through his nose.

"No, I know," I said, "but this *does* look exactly like a desktop background."

"This looks exactly like a West Texas sunset."

"Yeah, but you know what I'm saying. When you use a computer at the library, their background is always something like a sunset in the desert." I wasn't explaining my point very well, but was also bothered by how Dad refused to acknowledge even a slight similarity between the view in front of us and the view placed on the backgrounds of library computers.

Laura popped her door and jumped out. "Whoa. Desktop background much?"

I laughed but Dad ignored her. He walked ahead of us to read the signs pointing toward different lodges.

"Dad's become one with nature," I told Laura.

"Of course he has."

"I'd like to become one with dinner," I said.

"I'd like to take a number one and then have dinner," she said.

"I'd like to have dinner and then take a number two."

"That's disgusting."

"You started it," I argued.

"Well, you killed it."

We both looked toward Dad, who had just licked his finger and stuck it into the air.

"Does he think he's taking the temperature?" Laura said.

"I think he just likes licking his finger," I said.

"You're probably right."

"I think he's still mad at you, by the way," I said.

She shrugged. "Yeah, well, I'm mad at him, so I don't care."

"He was just teasing," I said.

"No, he wasn't. Just because he says something in the tone of a joke doesn't mean it's a joke. And physically putting his hand over my mouth to stop me from talking is *not* a joke."

"I thought it was funny," I said.

"Shut up," she said.

Dad turned in our direction as Laura punched me in the shoulder. He shook his head disapprovingly. "Let's start unpacking. Our lodge is a mile down that way," he said, pointing to a dusty path dwarfed by yellow grass.

We dragged our bags, the tent, and the cooler out from the car. Tomorrow was going to be our one camping night, and Dad wanted to bring everything we needed so we didn't have to trek back to the parking lot in the morning.

The lodge was a good choice for our first night. Though we'd all watched the same YouTube tutorials for how to properly set up a tent and cook food over controlled fire pits, we'd never actually done it together. Laura was a distinctly indoor person. She wasn't a Girl Scout and, as far as I knew, had never been camping. While I believed in her ability to long-term plan, I didn't know how much I could trust her hiking and navigating-nature abilities.

For most of my life, Dad casually appreciated nature on his own. As a high school science teacher, he has always been familiar with the scientific names for plants and animals, but he didn't usually make me go outside and listen to him as he said them.

After Mom died, though, he started watching shows about people stranded in the wilderness or thrown into the forest without supplies. Then he bought hiking boots and asked me if I wanted to go on walks with him around the Greenbelt in downtown Austin. I didn't and said no, but that didn't stop him. He went online and found a group of other men who'd watched the same shows and bought the same boots and were happy to go walking around in nature with him. His formerly iron grip on his wallet began to give way as he spent more and more money on outdoor gear. Slowly but surely over the past year and a half, he had completed his transformation into a Nature Dad. But there's a big difference between going on walks in the woods and maneuvering mountain paths in the desert.

I was a Cub Scout until I turned ten, but not a good one. I earned only seven badges in three years and they were the easy ones, like fishing. Even then, I never caught the required two fish. I just found a dead fish floating in the shallow end of a stream and took it up to the Scoutmaster twice over the course of several hours.

The yearly camping trips were always at lodges with bunk beds. The adults brought the food, made the fires, and cooked. There were activities where we had to go into the woods with compasses and find things, but I had a group of friends who'd hide out for an appropriate amount of time and then wander back, having found nothing. The adults didn't seem to care. Most of them were drinking and not paying attention.

My only *real* camping experience came during my one week as a Boy Scout. At Boy Scout camp, there were no lodges or bunk beds. On the first day, in a dirt patch in the middle of the forest, everyone had to find a partner and pitch a tent.

I knew immediately that this was not the place for me. I had been in Cub Scouts only because everyone else was, and I had decided to continue in Boy Scouts only because Seymour, my then-best-friend, was. During that first day in the woods, Seymour completely ditched me to hang out with the older kids.

They had snuck in a big box of cigarettes, kept swiping beers from their dads, and acted all mature, telling dirty jokes and talking about high school. To Seymour and the rest of my former Cub Scout troop, they were the coolest. But I didn't buy it. I never liked when someone acted better than me just because they were older. Being in high school is not cooler than being in middle school. It just means you have become the age where you have to go to high school.

I tried to say this to Seymour, but he said I was being "stuck-up" and kept hanging out with the older kids anyways. The only time we spent together was at night, when he'd come into the tent to sleep and pretend I wasn't there. I tried not to cry until after he fell asleep.

When Dad came to pick me up at the end of the week (Mom was sick at the time and not usually along for car rides, which may also explain some, but not all, of the crying), I told him I was ready to quit Boy Scouts. He argued with me a little but said it was fine as long as I called the Scoutmaster myself and told him why I wanted to quit. He said I should mention the drinking and smoking, but I didn't want to rat anyone out. The Scoutmaster's son had—surprise—been the worst of the bunch and could/would beat me up.

I called the Scoutmaster and told him that the wilderness was not the place for me. I was a modern boy who found comfort indoors and appreciated nature without having to conquer it. He responded with a string of insults, using language I was not expecting, but ultimately agreed that if I wanted out, good riddance. And so I was set free, returned from Boy Scout to boy, but left with the belief that little good can come from the outdoors.

Which is why spending the first night in Big Bend in a lodge —one with air conditioning, two beds, a shower, and a microwave—was a good way to ease into a week in the wilderness.

Over a dinner of microwaved hot dogs and Goldfish, Laura argued that she, as the only woman on the trip, deserved her own bed. Dad said that she was a girl, not yet a woman, sang a little bit of a Britney Spears song, and then agreed. So when it came time to sleep on the two queen-size beds with scratchy blankets draped over them, there was no disagreement. Dad and I went to one scratchy bed and Laura went to the other.

# TEN

**WHEN I WOKE UP** the next morning, the first thing I saw was Laura sitting on the floor next to the only outlet, furiously typing on her phone. I looked next to me and Dad was gone.

"Where's Dad?"

She didn't look up. "He left."

"Why didn't you guys wake me up?"

"I'm not a guy," she said, still not looking up. "He said he was going to drive back to Austin today to teach us a lesson about survival."

"WHAT?" I was now fully awake.

"I'm kidding. Calm down," she said, laying her phone on the floor to continue charging. "He's getting breakfast at the Visitor Center. He said to let you sleep until he got back. So I did. You're welcome."

"Thank you," I said. "I'm going back to sleep."

She threw a pillow at my face. "Don't you want to know what we're doing today?"

"No," I said. "I know you have it all planned out, but I don't care."

"You don't even care that I think I figured out the big surprise?" she asked, eyes widening.

"I'm listening," I said. I hadn't put much thought into the surprise because Dad had surprised us only once before. And that was the decision to come to Big Bend, which, so far, was an okay-to-maybe-bad surprise. I expected the other surprise would also be okay-to-bad.

"So, we know we're only spending four nights in the park. And we just spent one. So we only have three more nights here."

"Great job so far," I said.

"Shut up, I'm just getting started," she said. "I looked up other places in the area where we could possibly go and there's kind of nothing. There's a big telescope thing about an hour away but it's expensive and you can't camp there. There's Marfa, but that's, like, an art community and Dad doesn't understand art so that's also out."

"So you *didn't* figure it out," I said.

"Stop interrupting!" she said. "I was *having trouble* figuring it out, but then I had a realization. Instead of looking for the answer *online,* I should look for the answer in Dad's *stuff.* So I went through his backpack—and look at this!"

She handed me a printed-out reservation for two small houses right outside the park. The cost for two nights was over $300.

"Three hundred dollars?!" I said.

"I know," she said.

"Why would he . . ." It was difficult to form words after seeing Dad's name attached to such a high price.

"Not just why, but why *two houses?*" Laura said.

"I didn't even think about that part," I said.

"There's no way he's getting two houses just for us, right?" Laura said. "And the only possible person he would invite is Craig. So I went on Craig's Facebook—"

"You still have Facebook?" I said.

"Shut up. Just *listen*," she said. "I went on Craig's Facebook and his birthday is next week. I think—"

The sound of footsteps crunching toward the front door stopped Laura midsentence. I tossed the paper back to her, and she quickly jammed it into Dad's bag as he burst through the door in full wilderness gear—hiking boots, those pants with fifty pockets, and a sweat-proof shirt completely drenched in sweat. In his hands were three small cardboard boxes of, I hoped, breakfast food.

"L-O-L, Dad," Laura said. "Did you catch our breakfast from the river?"

"I think my sweat is too powerful for sweat-proof material," he said, wiping his sweaty head with his sweaty arm. "But 'thank' and 'you' are the only words I should be hearing from you two. I've already walked two miles so you could wake up to a warm breakfast."

"Thanks," I said, getting up to take my box back to bed.

"*Thank* and *you*," Laura said.

All three boxes were packed to the brim with every possible

breakfast option — pancakes, bacon, sausage, and eggs stacked in layers with a biscuit resting on top. If this was camping life, it wasn't so bad.

# ELEVEN

**AS SOON AS WE STEPPED OUTSIDE,** I learned that I was wrong. Camping life was extremely bad. The air conditioning inside the lodge had disguised the fact that it was 102 degrees outside. There were no clouds, no trees, and after five minutes I already felt like I'd been sunburned on my face, neck, arms, shoulders, and legs.

The sun wasn't the only concern. At the start of the trail stood a large warning sign that read THIS IS BEAR COUNTRY and listed tips for what to do when you saw a bear. Which you would because this was their country.

I'd read a book about a family that was eaten by bears, so I knew a little about the subject. From the book, it seemed that if a bear wanted to eat you, it would, and you'd die inside the bear's stomach. Dad waved this off and said we didn't have to worry because he bought something at the Visitor Center called bear spray. If a bear came near us, Dad would wait until it was within spraying distance and then spray the whole can in the bear's face.

Would this kill the bear? No.

Would it make the bear curl up into a little ball? No.

Would it make the bear angry but temporarily blind so we could run away if it didn't wildly swing its large claws around and slice us up anyways? Maybe, yes.

Dad said that if the one can of bear spray didn't work, we didn't have to worry, because he had a backup plan: another can of bear spray.

Laura pointed out that while bears were the only animals worthy of posted warnings, there were also several poisonous snakes in the area. And, at night, this part of the Chihuahuan Desert was famous for its "roving tarantula population."

I wished she had told me this earlier, because while I was expecting it to be hot, and for the days to be kind of long and maybe a little boring, I didn't know every step would be a battle for my continued existence.

If I was going to die now, at the tender age of thirteen, I didn't want it to be while hiking, because no one would be surprised. I was a known not-outdoors person. If I died, the news story wouldn't be "Theo Ripley unexpectedly passed away today doing what he loved: exploring the Texas wilderness." It would be "Theo Ripley attempted his first hike today and has, obviously, died. His family, saddened but not shocked, will continue with day two of their hiking plans."

But I didn't say any of this out loud. I took my spot as the last person in the line that started with Dad, bravely leading the way with spiked walking sticks, which, he promised, would keep away the snakes and tarantulas as effectively as the bear spray kept away the bears.

Laura, second in line, didn't have walking sticks but was otherwise prepared with newish sneakers that had enough traction on the bottom to prevent her from falling off a mountain.

I had on basketball shoes a little bit older than hers, which didn't have that much traction but were comfortable and broken in. In addition to my backpack, I had our small cooler slung over my shoulder. I figured that if I kept pace, stayed alert for snakes and tarantulas and bears, and avoided stepping along the edges of any mountains, I'd make it through the first day just fine.

Because Dad had drunk three cups of coffee at the Visitor Center, we started at a ridiculously fast pace. Coffee generally made him insane and he led us forward like a superhero walking through walls. He was high-knee stomping, swinging his hiking sticks back and forth, and yelling things over his shoulder like "Here we go!" and "Mush! Mush!" It made me feel like a dog on a leash being dragged up a hill by an abusive owner.

With each inclined step, I began to hate him more and more. But I knew his coffee power lasted only a few hours and he'd soon turn back into the science teacher who wanted to pause every few minutes to discuss the genera of the plants he was destroying with his walking sticks.

The explosive pace also made the first stretch of our hike seem shorter than it really was. The Chisos Trail starts in the middle of a mountain and then continues upward for several miles. The higher we climbed, the more intensely the sun burned, and the thinner the air became. It wasn't very long before I was panting and exclusively breathing through my open mouth.

Every fifteen minutes or so we passed resting sections with signs pointing toward different, seemingly easier paths, but Dad insisted that we needed to keep following the same path without breaks. If we "kept pushing," we'd soon be rewarded.

After nearly two hours of zigging and zagging upward through rocks, the reward finally came. Lagging slightly behind Dad and Laura, I stumbled over the last dusty rock at the peak of the path and stepped into a wide green meadow. Green! With flowers and trees and everything. I thought that maybe I was dazed by the sun and had started to hallucinate, but I ran my fingers through the tall grass and confirmed that it was real.

I lurched under a tree to enjoy the very real shade and dumped my backpack and the cooler onto the ground. The speed and purpose of our first spurt had kept me from focusing on the pain coursing through my body. But as soon as I sat down I noticed that my shoulders hurt, my legs hurt, my shirt was plastered to my body with sweat, and I needed to drink so much water.

Laura must have felt the same sudden fatigue, because she quickly collapsed into a pile next to the cooler before moving into the shade and resting her head against the tree trunk.

Dad, on the last of his caffeinated fumes, continued acting like a Discovery Channel host astonished by every detail of the land.

"How. About. This," he said, slowly spinning around with open arms. "Now *this* is better than any desktop background. Am I right, Theo?"

"Right on, Dad," I said, too tired to offer anything else.

While scanning the horizon, "drinking in the vistas," Dad spotted a pair of hikers in the far distance. He told us it was proper hike etiquette to meet and greet travelers of the same trail. We were all brothers (and one sister) of Mother Nature now and had to show kindness to our kin. Those were his exact words. Nature had fully infected his brain and he had become Nature Dad.

We rested as he marched toward his new brothers. It was far away, but I could see the general outlines of two people, one slightly taller and rounder than the other. The taller and rounder person accepted Dad's handshake and then both hikers, following the direction of Dad's pointing, turned our way. They waved a friendly "hello" gesture but, thankfully, not a "come over" gesture, so we continued sitting.

"How much do you want to bet Dad is going to bring them over here?" I asked.

"Like, a real bet or are you just using that expression?" Laura said.

"A real bet," I said. "With money. I bet you five dollars that he brings them over here."

"No, because Dad will obviously bring them over here. And I don't have five dollars."

"How about one dollar, then," I said. "I bet you one dollar that Dad makes us go over there."

"Also no. Why do you want to bet anyways?"

"Because this is boring so far. We're just following Dad. It's one hundred ten degrees. We're not even stopping to look at anything. So why not make it interesting? I bet you one dollar that Dad waves us over there. If he doesn't, you get a dollar."

"I mean, I guess," she said. "You're going to lose. And I don't have a dollar. So even if you win, you won't make any money. But I'll take the bet."

Almost immediately, Dad and his two new Mother Nature brothers started walking toward us.

"You owe me a dollar," she said.

# TWELVE

**THE TWO STRANGERS** were now close enough to decipher as an older and younger man, probably father and son but possibly uncle and nephew or young grandpa and grandson. The older one and Dad were already deep in a lively conversation while the younger one kept a few paces behind.

He looked the way the Boy Scouts looked: in high school, tall, comfortable with hiking boots and camping gear, confidently striding, effortlessly showcasing all the things that I was not. Unlike the Boy Scouts, however, he had his phone out and paused every few steps to take a picture of himself sticking out his tongue. During the journey across the meadow, he took four different pictures of himself with his tongue out.

He was wearing sunglasses, but when he noticed Laura, he took them off and gave her a big smile. To my surprise, Laura responded by dusting off her pants and repositioning herself so it looked like she was resting on the earth in a meaningful yoga pose instead of crashing on the ground from exhaustion.

"Here they are," Dad said, gesturing toward us, "my son, Theo, and my daughter, Laura."

"Hiii," Laura squealed.

"Hey," I said.

"And this is Leonard and his son, Leonard Jr.," Dad said.

"Leo," Leonard Jr. corrected.

"Hello, Leo," Laura said in, I guess, her flirting voice.

"It's Leonard Jr.," Leonard said, shooting a warning look at his son. "And I'm Leonard Blenard. Pleased to meet you."

"Your name is Leonard Blenard?" I asked.

"Yes," Leonard said. "And it's a fine name, much like your own. Theo, was it?"

"Uh-huh," I said.

Leonard turned toward Dad. "Was he perhaps named after former president Theodore Roosevelt?"

"People often think that," Dad said. "But he's actually named after another Theo. Theodore Maiman. The inventor of the laser."

"Pew pew," I said, fake-shooting a laser gun in Leonard's direction, which usually got a laugh.

Leonard stared at me in confusion for a few seconds before continuing, "Well, I'll be. And I suppose Laura here is named after the inventor of the flying saucer?"

"Ha, but no. After Laura Ingalls Wilder," Dad said. "My wife liked those books. The *Little House on the Prairie* books."

"And where is your wife?" Leonard asked.

Dad briefly shuddered before putting on his usual smile. "She, uh, couldn't make it."

"A shame," Leonard said.

"But what about Leonard Jr.," Dad said, quickly changing the subject. "He was named after . . . you?"

"Myself, yes," Leonard said. "My former wife, his mother,

wanted to call him Wallace or some such, but I said no, this here is Leonard Jr. I signed the birth certificate before she could disagree further. He's been rejecting 'Junior' lately, going by *Leo* and whatnot, but it's just a phase. You know how these things go."

"It's not a phase," Leo said.

"Well," Dad said, turning toward Laura and me, "Leonard and Leonard Jr. here—"

"Leo," Leonard Jr. corrected again.

"*Leo* and Leonard here are some real, bona fide nature experts, and they've offered—"

"To join camps for the day," Leonard interrupted. "Combine traveling parties. I think we could help each other out. I am, among other things, an amateur ornithologist."

He paused, waiting for us to ask him what that meant. We didn't.

"You may be wondering what this is . . ." he offered.

We weren't and remained quiet, but that didn't discourage him.

"Well, I'll just go ahead and tell you, then. It is, in simplest terms, the study of birds. Some call it birdwatching, but I don't just watch. I also examine and photograph. My son is my partner."

"I'm not his partner," Leo said, scrolling through pictures on his phone.

"He sure is," Leonard said, reaching over to put his hand on Leo's shoulder. Leo immediately shrugged it off and slunk several steps away.

"He's a jokester, this one," Leonard said with a weak smile. "Anyways, your father said he's quite the nature fan himself and would be happy to spend some time this afternoon tracking down the elusive Colima warbler and some of her other feathered friends. And if all five of us were working together, just think of how many friends we'd be able to find." He leaned forward with a large grin that was meant to be inviting but instead looked deranged.

"Well, what do you think?" Dad asked, also grinning.

Laura eyed Leo. "Let's do it," she said.

"What?" I accidentally shouted, genuinely surprised.

"Let's watch some birds," Laura said. "It's better than watching Dad's butt walk up a mountain."

"What's wrong with my butt?" Dad asked.

"Your butt's fine, Dad," I said. "But what about the rest of our plans for today?" I said to Laura. "The ones *you* made?"

"Who cares," Laura said. "We're already not following them. So let's watch some birds."

"This is a *serious* yes?" Dad said.

"Yes!" Laura said. "I'm agreeing to join the amateur orny-whatevers."

"Ornithologists," Leonard clarified.

"Theo?" Dad asked.

"Whatever," I said. "Yes, I guess."

Did I really want to join the father and son birdwatching duo where the father called birds his friends and the son was Laura's new boyfriend after five minutes? Of course not. But that's the plight of being the younger brother and baby of the family. Your opinion can be expressed, but it doesn't actually matter. Adults and older sisters always win.

"Splendid," Leonard said, taking a heavily creased bird map out of his back pocket. "The day is still young."

# THIRTEEN

**LEONARD WAS ON** what he called his Big Year. It's the title that bird weirdos use to describe the year of their life they dedicate to finding and photographing as many different native North American bird species as possible. The record is 784. So far, Leonard had found and photographed 486 birds. With six months remaining, he was confident that he'd make it to 785, a new world record, by the end of the year.

Leo was on what he called his Legally Required Summer with His Birth Father. It's the title he used to describe the two months of the year he's forced to spend with his dad in Texas. This was the third summer since his parents' divorce and the second in which his dad would only talk to him about birds.

How did I know all this? Because I was stuck between the two split groups. Dad and Leonard were ahead of me discussing birds, and Laura and Leo were behind discussing how Leo hated his dad and Laura hated our dad. I was just a receptor, listening to both conversations simultaneously, tuning in or out depending on interest. Most of the time, both conversations were uninteresting.

After an hour of walking, sweating, and twice stopping to increase Leonard's bird count, we emerged onto a clearing that led to the edge of the mountain we'd been scaling. I immediately recognized it as the view from the cover of the official Big Bend booklet. I cautiously approached the edge, careful to not stumble off.

The sight was undeniably beautiful. Beneath the bluest possible sky, dark brown mountain peaks stretched upward from the valley below. Real-deal mountains, not little Austin mountains, or mounds of mud with patches of grass, but the kind of immense, awe-inspiring mountains I'd seen only on IMAX screens and Instagram.

I sat down to take a picture as both sides of the hiking party erupted in their own ways.

**DAD:** Breathtaking.
**LEONARD:** Magnificent.
**DAD:** Can you believe it?
**LEONARD:** Can *you* believe it?
**DAD:** I can't. I just can't believe it.
**LEONARD:** I think I can, but—

As they continued discussing whether or not the view could be believed, I shifted my attention to Laura and Leo.

**LEO:** This is it. *This* is that SP I've been waiting for.
**LAURA:** *SP?*
**LEO:** Sick pic. You know, a picture that'll get, like, massive engagement.
**LAURA:** Do you even get service up here?

**LEO:** Here? No. Two to six isn't a good time to post anyways. But there's enough service at the campsite to drop this in prime time.

**LAURA:** I didn't know you were such an Instagram expert.

**LEO:** I have a pretty effective social media strategy. Instagram's just one part of the empire. My engagement numbers are at an all-time high across platforms.

**LAURA:** And how high is that?

**LEO:** You know, like four hundred views. Five hundred sometimes. If you got in on this pic, I bet I could get up to six hundred. What do you think? You wanna get in on this pic?

**LAURA:** Um . . . I mean, I guess.

**LEO:** What's your brother's name again?

"Theo! Theo, come here!" Laura called, interrupting my eavesdropping and forcing me to join the conversation.

"You want me to take an SP of you with the mountains in the background?" I asked.

"Don't listen to my private conversations!" Laura said.

"What else am I supposed to do? I left my earbuds in the lodge. The dads are taking turns saying '*I can't believe it*,'" I said in a pitch-perfect Leonard impression.

"That sounds like Leonard, all right," Leo said.

"Why, exactly, do you call your dad Leonard?" Laura said.

"Doesn't it seem like a cliché—a teenager calling his dad by his first name to annoy him?"

"It might be a cliché, but he still hates it. Try calling your dad by his real name. The first couple times he'll get really angry, but then he'll just give up and accept it. It rules."

"Our dad's actually not that bad," I said.

"Yes, he is. Stanley—*that's our dad's name*," Laura whispered to Leo, "skipped all of my plans, made none himself besides a surprise that he still hasn't explained at all, and only pretends to let us have a say in what we're doing."

"Okay, yeah, for two days he hasn't been great," I said. "But that doesn't make him a bad person."

"We don't have to decide if your dad is good or bad right now," Leo cut in. "But we should probably snap that pic."

"You'll take it?" Laura asked me.

"Fine," I said. "Dad's mostly fine and I'll take your picture."

Leo gave me his phone, and the two of them began maneuvering through all the classic poses: side by side with arms around each other's shoulders, squatting with prayer hands, and backs turned, gazing appreciatively at the sights before them.

It was difficult to tell if Leo was just using her to show off for his "fans" and gain more likes by appearing to have a new girlfriend, or if he genuinely liked her and was using this as an excuse to keep putting his arm around her shoulders. I would need to discreetly find and comb through his Instagram later to see if posing with girls in exotic locations was a common theme.

It was also difficult to understand why Laura was going along with any of this. She wasn't the kind of person who would willingly spend time with someone who dissected their social media engagement numbers. It could've been because he was older. I had already seen the power that older guys seemed to have over people in younger grades. There were people in my class who were going out with freshmen in high school simply because they were freshmen in high school. I thought it was dumb, but I also don't know the feeling of being wanted by an older person. Or a younger person. Or someone my own age. So, ultimately, I cannot judge.

"Thanks a lot, man," Leo said, yanking his phone from my hands and rapidly scrolling through the fifty pictures I'd taken in one minute. "This is great stuff. You have a real eye. I'll tease some of these in my Stories and drop the best one tonight. This one right here."

"Can I see?!" Laura squeezed next to him, snatching the phone from his hand. "Aw, this one is really good. Can you send this to me?"

"I'd have to get your number first," Leo disgustingly teased.

"I guess I'll have to put it in your phone," Laura sickeningly countered.

"Okay, bye," I said, walking up to the higher plane at the very edge of the mountain, where Dad and Leonard were doing their own, old-men version of posing: hands on hips, snapping shots from bad angles that blocked the view of the mountains they were trying to capture.

"Theo, just the man we were looking for," Dad said. "Can you take our picture?"

Maybe I should give up drawing and become a professional photographer. I nodded yes. Dad passed me his phone and Leonard gave me his camera.

They continued standing next to each other with their hands on their hips.

"How does it look?" Leonard asked.

They looked like two dads on a mountain, sweating.

"Perfect," I said.

I returned Dad's phone and Leonard's camera and they both started checking my work. As Dad scrolled through his pictures, his face fell. He started lightly pressing on his stomach and asked, "Do you think I've been gaining weight?"

"What?" I said.

"Do you think my stomach's gotten a little . . . *larger* lately?" Dad asked.

"Um, I don't think so," I said. "You look the same to me." I'd never contemplated Dad's physical appearance because he'd looked the same since the day I was born.

"Your stomach is fine, my friend," Leonard assured him, holding his own portly stomach with both hands. "This," he said, "is a belly. If you can't do this"—he shook his stomach and watched it jiggle around in front of him—"then you're a skinny man."

Dad ran both of his hands over his stomach and indeed couldn't grab ahold of it and make it dance around like Leonard's.

"You see?" Leonard said. "You don't have a belly."

Dad looked relieved.

I glanced back at Laura and Leo to see if I could escape the belly-shaking dad party and join them, but Leo was now posing solo with Laura as his personal photographer. I contemplated what I had done in my life to deserve this. Over the course of one morning, my summer vacation had become Boy Scout camp all over again. Everyone else had found a new friend, and I was left alone to watch them having their versions of fun.

"So," I interrupted the middle-aged-men weight discussion. "Are we hiking more or stopping to rest or—"

"A good question," Leonard started.

"I was more asking my dad," I said.

"It's okay. I'd like to hear what Leonard has to say," Dad said.

"I'd like to hear what *you* have to say," I said.

"If I may, I'll have my say now and then you can each have your own say," Leonard said. "It's approaching five. We're about two miles from the campsite and there's more than enough space to fit another tent if you'd like to join us for the night. After setting up camp and eating dinner, there should still be enough light for some evening birding. What do you think?"

"We'll take it," Dad said immediately.

"You don't want to ask Laura?" I said.

"She seems like she's having a good time with Leo. I don't think she'll mind."

"Well, what if *I* mind?"

"Do you mind?" Dad asked.

"Yeah, a little. I mean, this isn't exactly what I'd like to be doing. You're having fun. Laura's having fun. I'm . . . sweating and . . . listening to other people having fun."

"You can hike up front with Leonard and me if you want."

"That's not what I mean."

Dad put on his concerned "listening" voice. "What can I do to make sure you have a better time?"

"I don't know. Find some more shade? Stop hiking? Go home?"

"We're only two more miles to the campsite," Leonard added. "I guarantee you'll find some shade there until the sun settles her head for the night."

"See?" Dad said. "We're almost done. And like I said, you can hike with us for the last two miles. Does that sound better?"

"Not really."

"Come on, Theo."

"I mean, I'll do it. There aren't any other options. But don't think you've convinced me."

"Sounds all settled," Leonard said. "Now let's move. Feet forward but eyes open. We must remain ready for any bird that could appear upon our path."

I angrily stared at Dad. He smiled back at me, gave an encouraging double thumbs-up, and turned to follow Leonard.

# FOURTEEN

**THE CAMPSITE WAS** a grassless patch of dirt beneath dying trees. But there *was* shade, and a sun-warped picnic table, and a scorched grill that looked like it would dissolve into dust with the gentlest kick.

"Home sweet home," Dad said, setting down his backpack and the carrying case that held Craig's tent.

"Tonight we sleep with the dirt as our pillow and the stars as our ceiling," Leonard said. "Do you know who said that?"

It hadn't been a fun time walking with them for the past hour.

"Johnny Appleseed?" Dad guessed.

"No. Another guess?"

"Davy Crockett?" Dad guessed again.

"Not quite," Leonard said. "A final guess?"

"You?" I guessed.

"Ding, ding, ding! We have a winner!" Leonard gushed. "It was me. It's my own quotation."

"Cool, Leonard," Leo said, tossing his own bag onto the ground. "Now I'm gonna quote myself. Are you ready? Quote —start making dinner."

"I will under one condition: you stop calling me Leonard.

Can you do that? Just practice—*Dad, can you please start making dinner?*"

"Okay, Leonard. *Dad, can you start making dinner?*"

"Close enough. I'll get the grill going."

Leonard methodically disassembled his backpack and produced a bag of coal and matches. It seemed incredibly dangerous to carry a bag of coal and matches on your back in 110-degree heat, but Leonard hadn't burst into flames, so I guess it's fine. As he got the grill going, Leo led Laura through setting up the two tents.

Neither Leonard nor Leo seemed like the "bona fide nature experts" Dad made them out to be, but they'd certainly camped before. Leo knew how to drive nails into the ground to keep the tents secure and Leonard knew how to lay chicken onto a grill. This was more than Dad had proven capable of. His greatest nature skill so far had been finding another family that could provide us with food and shelter.

As everyone else was busy enjoying themselves, I moved to the picnic table and turned my phone back on to see if I had any service. It was only one bar but enough for a text to come through:

**ANGEL P.:** hows the park?
**ME:** Kind of cool, kind of boring

I sent my response but got back an error message. I pressed

send again with the same result. I moved away from the picnic table and in a little loop to see if it would go through, but no luck.

I took out my notebook and continued working on *Bob: The Boy with Perfect Memory*. I hadn't done any work so far on the trip, so I was still at the part where Bob is deciding whether or not to take the pill that would give him an average human memory. The scientist explains that if Bob takes the pill, his complete second-by-second recall of the worst moments of his life will slowly fade from his mind.

On a new page, I drew an outline of Bob's head and the three worst moments of his life. By far, the worst moment of his life is the day his mother died. I took out the picture that Mrs. Stilden had given me before we left and placed it next to my notebook.

Using the picture as a guide, I drew Bob's mother's smiling face on top of a body lying in a hospital bed. Then I drew a series of panels that show Bob trying to fall asleep every night as the image of his mom in a hospital bed invades his mind.

The scientist tries to explain the science behind the pill, but Bob isn't listening. On a new page, I drew Bob pondering his decision and trying to decide if he wants the memory of his mother's last day alive diminished, maybe even completely erased. In his mind, Bob envisions a carefree life where he wakes up to a smiling sun every day and quickly falls asleep under a smiling moon every night.

Bob interrupts the scientist's explanation and says yes, he'll take the pill. He wants to become Bob: The Boy with Normal Memory.

The scientist clasps his hands together in delight.

As I started to draw the scientist's excited face, my concentration was broken by the sound of a spoon clanging against a pan. Startled by the sudden noise, I instinctively flinched and my pencil snapped against my notebook.

"Dinner is served!" Leonard hollered while continuing to bang the spoon against the pan.

I looked down at my broken pencil and sighed. I would have been mad if I weren't so hungry. I closed my notebook, slipped it into my backpack, and joined the feast of lightly burned chicken.

# FIFTEEN

**AFTER DINNER,** Leonard and Dad went on a sunset bird-spotting stroll while I was stuck with Leo and Laura. They were sitting at the picnic table whispering back and forth. It seemed like she had mostly gotten sick of him by this point but had remained by his side to pass the time.

Ordinarily, I would have left them alone, gone into the tent, and continued drawing. But there wasn't any light in the tent, I'd drawn as much as I wanted to for the day, and I was tired of being on the outside of conversations. I walked over and sat next to Laura.

"Um, hi," Laura said. "There isn't another piece of wood where you can sit?"

I glared at her.

"It's okay," Leo said. "We were actually just going to come find you."

"We were?" Laura asked.

"I was," he said. "I could use those cameraman skills of yours again if you don't mind."

"You couldn't find a sick enough pic?" I asked.

"I've got more SPs than I know what to do with. But you know that's only one side of the enterprise. I also have my You-Tube channel to update."

Laura was shocked. "You have a *YouTube channel?*"

"Of course. I can't build my brand through only one medium. Everyone knows you have to diversify across multiple platforms."

Laura put on an extremely strained smile. "Great point," she said, her interest in Leo immediately waning from her eyes. She mostly hated YouTubers and now that Leo had identified himself as such, his entire personality made sense.

"The only reason I come on these dumb trips is for the views. If I thumbnail a video with some trees in the background? *Automatically* five hundred more views."

"Cool," she said unenthusiastically.

"I can shoot your video if you have a phone," I said. "Mine's essentially dead."

"Isn't your phone nearly dead too?" Laura asked Leo, having helped him edit, filter, and post pictures for the past hour.

"My TikTok and Instagram phone is almost dead. But that's why I have this one" — he pulled out a sleek new iPhone — "for YouTube."

"Do you have a Snapchat phone in another pocket?" I said.

"No way. Snapchat sucks."

"Oh yeah, ha-ha." I had Snapchat despite barely using it. I had Instagram, too, but only fifty-six friends and twelve posted photos. My most liked photo was a drawing of a pizza where the pepperonis are giving each other high-fives. It has fourteen likes, but four of them were from extended family members, which doesn't really count. "I can film your video if you tell me where to point the camera."

"Awesome. Thanks, man. Just point the camera at my face. I'm the star of the show."

"Great," I said as he handed me his YouTube phone.

"Laura, do you want to be in the intro or can I bring you in later?" Leo asked.

"How about I'm not in any part of it?" she said.

"Come on. My fans already saw you on the Stories. They want to see what's going on between us."

"But nothing *is* going on between us."

"I don't know about that."

"I do."

"You're hurting my feelings here," Leo said, pressing his hand to his heart while making a wounded face. "How about this: at the very end, I'll cut over to you and you pretend like you just finished setting up the tent."

"Are you going to imply that we're *sharing* a tent?"

"No, come on. Total respect. I'll show you as a totally strong, independent woman. You're the one taking charge and keeping us, you know, tented. Protected in a tent. It's feminist."

"You're confused about the meaning of feminism, but yes, fine. If you'll stop talking, then I'll pretend to set up a tent."

"I knew you'd come around." Leo winked at Laura, who grimaced. "All right, let's get this set up," he continued. "Should I be here at the picnic table or should I be, like, in front of a tree?"

"I think the light is good here," I said.

"My hair?"

It looked bad from wearing a hat all day. "Great," I said.

"All right, let me get some moisture," he said, and aggressively licked his lips. "Good to go. Fire it up."

I tilted the phone sideways, pressed the record button, and gestured for Leo to start.

"What's up, Leo Babies. We're out here—"

"Ewwww," Laura interrupted. "You call your viewers *Leo Babies?*"

"Baebies. Like *b-a-e.*"

"That's even worse," she said.

"It's not—look, people like it. Don't interrupt me when I'm in the flow. Theo, are we good to go again?"

I gave him the thumbs-up and he sprang back into action: "What's up, Leo Baebies. How's it going? How *you* doing? You already know where we are. We're back out here in the wild for the next couple days. If you're not subscribing, you're gonna be mad missing out. So why don't you go ahead and SMASH that subscribe button! And, cut."

"You want me to stop?" I asked.

"Yeah, cut here and let's switch it up. I want to be by that tree for the next part."

He walked over to a large tree and squatted down next to it. It cast a shadow across most of his face. "How does it look?" he asked.

"Perfect," I said.

"Then fire it back up!"

I tilted the phone and zoomed in on his face.

"So, yo, you've seen my Stories — you know I'm back out here in Mother Nature with my birth father and legal parent, Leonard." He pretended to push glasses up his nose and started speaking in a high-pitched "nerd" voice. "*I think I can hear the blue-footed booby. No, wait, that's the red-boobied booty.* Ha-ha. He's out there sniffing bird poop right now. But we're here chilling. Big Bend National Park. Roll the footage. And, cut."

"You want me to stop again?" I asked.

"Yeah, cut there. I'll edit in the pictures. Put a hot song behind them. And now back on me. Rolling."

I pressed record again. "Fam, how sick are those sights? You don't even know. Like, unless you've been here, you don't even know. And if I can get serious here for a second. If I can just be really real here for just one moment. Standing up on those mountains, it made me feel, like, you know, important. Like I had really *done* something. You know what I mean? Like, this morning, when I was all the way down at the bottom, and I was looking up and I was like" — he bugged out his eyes and leaned into the camera — "*naaawwwwww. No way I can get up there. That's just too hiiigghhh.* But then I just started walking, putting one foot in front of the other, and before you know it, I was there. At the top. So — I don't know, just something to think about. Maybe if you have something in your life that looks like you can't do it. You can. If you just keep going, someday you'll be on top." He paused thoughtfully.

"Now, I've seen your comments and I know what you all've been thinking." He put his hands on both cheeks and started talking in an even-higher-pitched "female voice." *"Oh my god. Who's that girl? When did he meet her? What's her deal? Why is she so cute? Who is it? WHO IS IT?"* He laughed at himself and returned to his normal voice. "Calm down, calm down. She's not my new *girl*. She's just, you know, a *friend*." He leaned in and slowly winked for his Leo Baebies. "We're" — he winked again — *"friendly."* Wink, wink. "And she's a real wilderness girl. You were raised by wolves, right?"

Laura didn't say anything.

"You said you'd be in the video. Come on," Leo said.

"I said I'd pretend to set up the tent, not talk," Laura said.

"But you should talk, too. Just a little. Just, like, answer my questions."

Laura glared at him for several seconds and then, through gritted teeth, said, "Fine."

"Let's keep rolling," Leo said. "I'll pick up where I left off. When I ask Laura a question, move over to her so she can answer. Got it?"

"Yeah," I said.

"So listen, she's a real wilderness girl. You were raised by wolves, right?"

I moved the phone to capture Laura sitting next to the tent, scowling. "No."

"Ha-ha, she's playing. You were raised by bears?"

"No," Laura sullenly replied again.

"She's funny. She's funny. Well, it looks like she has our tent all set up." Another wink. "I'm about to crash for the night, if you know what I mean. Come on, no dirty thoughts, guys, nothing dirty is happening. If you want to see the next step in the Big Bend adventure, hit that subscribe, hit that like, stay tuned to the world's best YouTube channel. It's your boy Leo, ow, ow, ouutttt. And, cut. What did you think?"

"No comment," I said.

"No comment," Laura said.

# SIXTEEN

**FOR THREE PEOPLE,** our tent was pretty small. There was enough room for a row of three sleeping bags with two inches between them, but little else. For one night, however, it was acceptable.

I was so tired from the heat, and from Leo, and his dad, and my dad, and Laura, that I fell asleep almost immediately. Even the fear that a snake would somehow wiggle under our tent and pierce its fangs through the lining to strike me directly in the neck like a vampire could not slow the momentum of exhaustion from speeding me into sleep.

But it was not such a deep sleep that I wasn't woken by a mysterious rustling against the side of the tent. It was a sound beyond wind and closer to a gentle clawing by animal paw or person. A sound that terrified me into doing the immediate mental calculations of what, exactly, it could be.

Snakes don't have hands so it was not, thankfully, a snake. That meant it could be a raccoon, squirrel, rabid raccoon or squirrel, misplaced pet dog, wild dog, rabid dog, deer, Lyme-diseased deer, aardvark, anteater, tarantula, mountain lion, or bear. I was hoping for an anteater. They seem fairly chill and interested only in killing ants.

I lay petrified and alone in my terror. The rising and falling of Laura's and Dad's sleeping bags confirmed they were still asleep, and I didn't want to wake them if it *was* just an anteater. For a few seconds there was silence. Then the sound of something rearranging its position on the ground and another light clawing against the tent. Laura bolted forward out of her sleeping bag.

"What was that?" she whisper-yelled.

"I don't know," I whispered back. "It's the second time, though. Whatever it is."

"Should we wake Dad up?" she asked.

From outside, a low voice whispered, "Don't wake Daddy."

Laura instinctively swung her hand in the direction of the voice. Her open palm connected with a slight pop, and the person outside produced a muffled grunt and wincing curses.

Dad slowly rolled over but remained asleep, his lips parted and gently snoring.

"That really hurt," Laura whispered while shaking out her right hand.

"I think it worked," I said.

But after a few seconds of silence, the figure outside inched back toward the same area of the tent. Laura snapped both hands into a boxer pose, ready to strike.

"It's . . . Leo," the voice slowly enunciated. "Don't . . . hit me."

"You idiot!" Laura shrieked.

"Shhhh!" I said, eyeing still-snoring Dad.

"Is that Theo?" Leo asked, now apparently sticking around for a conversation.

"Yes, it's me," I whispered. "What did you expect? This is our tent. There's more than just Laura in here. Our dad's here too."

"For sure," Leo said. "For sure. No disrespect to you, Theo. Or to your dad. It's just—I wanted to talk to Laura. Like, privately. If you could, uh, not listen? Or maybe, Laura, if you could come outside so we don't have to keep whispering so much?"

"I'm staying here," Laura said.

"I'm listening," I said.

"Cool, cool. No worries," Leo said. "Well, I guess I just wanted to say what's up."

"It's two forty a.m.," Laura said.

"I'm a night owl, you caught me," he said. "I just wanted to, uh, you know, see if maybe you were a night owl too."

"Did you come over here to seduce my sister?" I asked.

"I don't know about *seduce*. Just to say what's up and see what's up—as I said."

"Well, I'm not a night owl," Laura said. "And I don't care what's up with you. I was asleep and I'm going back to sleep."

"Maybe you could just give me a little kiss before you go back to sleep. To heal my nose. You know, it really hurt when you hit me," he said, sounding genuinely hurt.

"No," Laura said.

"Aw, come on," he said. "I don't think my nose will recover without it."

"No! I'm not kissing your nose just because you're up late being gross and want an apology."

"You can't fault me for trying."

"I can," Laura said.

"I also think you're at fault," I added.

"I guess I'll go back to my tent, then," he said.

"Good night," Laura said.

"Good night. To Laura. Not to you, Theo."

"What did I do?" I said. But Leo was already gone.

# SEVENTEEN

**WHEN I WOKE UP** again, the tent was empty. I could smell frying bacon and eggs, which signaled Leonard was up and ready for a new day. I could faintly hear Leo making a Story about Leonard making breakfast. Closer to the tent, I could hear Laura and Dad whispering.

"I thought you and Leo were getting along," Dad said.

"Yeah, maybe for the first few hours," Laura said. "Before he kept talking and I heard the words he chose to say, the way he views the world, and the personality he's settled on. Then I stopped liking him."

"He's not *that* bad," Dad said. "He's just young."

"I'm younger than him and I'm not an idiot."

"I know you're very smart, Laura. It's one of the things I love most about you. But I also love how you can be accommodating and understanding of people who may be different than you. People who will maybe help us to see some aspects of nature that we wouldn't be able to find on our own?"

As Dad continued pleading with Laura, I heard the sound of snapping branches from the other side of the tent. I unzipped the netting and peered outside. My eyes immediately zeroed in on a black bear about five hundred feet away, clawing at the trunk of a tree.

For a few seconds I froze, unsure of what to do. I was kind of hoping that someone else would see it and take charge, but they were all too busy cooking and recording and talking to notice. I took a deep breath and quickly but quietly bolted out of the tent toward Laura and Dad.

"Dad! Dad!" I whisper-shouted. "Stop. Stop talking."

He turned around and I pressed my finger to my lips. Leonard and Leo looked over from their position by the grill.

"Hey, what's go—" Leonard started before noticing my raised finger.

Minutely moving my finger from the quiet signal, I pointed left. Their eyes followed the direction of my index finger to the bear, still clawing at the tree trunk.

Everyone started yelling at the same time.

**LAURA:** Jesus Christ!

**LEO:** (Curse!)

**DAD:** Spray! The spray! I have bear spray. We'll be fine . . . with the spray!

**LEONARD:** Get away, you beast!

"Shhhhhhhhhhh. Stop . . . yelling . . . please," I begged.

Dad started fishing around in his backpack for the bear spray, but everyone else stopped and listened.

"I actually," I whispered to the now attentive audience, "read a book about a family attacked by bears. So I kind of know what to do."

"I have the spray," Dad said, clutching both cans.

"We don't need the spray yet," I said. "It's a black bear. Black bears don't want to attack people. But it needs to know that we're, you know, people."

We all looked over at the bear, who had noticed that we were something. Its body was turned in our direction, eyes fixed on the grill.

"Well," Laura said in a panic, "what's the first step?"

"The first thing we need to do is talk. Quietly," I said, my voice shaking. "Not shouting, but like, normal talking. So, um, start talking."

They all started talking.

The bear continued looking in our direction but remained motionless below its neck.

"Is it good that it's looking at us?" Laura whispered.

"It's okay. It's just looking," I answered. "It's seeing us. It's seeing that we're people." Everyone but Leonard stopped talking to wait for the next instruction.

"Okay, now Leonard, shut up," I said.

"Well, excuse me, but—"

"Shut. Up," I said again.

He shut up.

"I need you to do the next step," I said.

Leonard silently nodded.

"*Carefully* pour some water on the food," I said.

He grabbed his canteen and slowly poured water onto the

sizzling grill. The flame sputtered out and sent a small plume of smoke into the air. The bear raised its head.

"That seems bad," Leo said.

"It's okay," I said. "It's just smelling the air, sensing a change. It knows we're people. And it's smelling that we don't have food anymore. I hope. Now we're supposed to, uh, show that we're people without food who don't want to harm it. So, um — wave your arms around a little. Slowly. To show that we're not dangerous."

Everyone but Leo began moving their arms around as if making snow angels in the air. Leo took out his phone and started filming the bear. The bear stood up on its hind legs, focusing its attention on Leo's phone.

"This seems *really* bad," Leo said.

"Wave your arms!" I said to Leo.

"Then the footage will be all shaky," Leo said.

"You don't need to record everything," Laura said.

"But this could be my last video ever," Leo said.

The bear, now fully standing up, began leaning its head in our direction and thrusting its nose forward. The twitching nose scared Leo into putting away his phone. He finally joined us in gently waving and the bear froze.

"What's the next step?" Dad asked.

"Just wait," I said. "It's okay. Keep waving your arms."

"What happens in the book?" Leonard asked.

"The bear kills the family," I said.

The bear crashed down onto all four paws.

"So maybe these are the wrong steps?" Laura said.

"No, these are the real ones. The ones in the back of the book about how to not get killed. Trust me."

"Are you a smart kid?" Leonard asked.

"He's smart," Dad said.

"He's okay," Laura said.

The bear lowered its head to the ground and inched toward us with stumbling steps.

"I still have the spray," Dad said.

"Just keep waving. Don't stop," I said.

The bear continued slowly pacing forward.

"Are there any other steps?!" Laura shouted.

"Um . . . no," I said.

"So what should we do?" Laura said.

"Just wait," I said.

The bear took another step forward. It opened its mouth and began clacking its teeth together.

"You're sure we shouldn't run?" Dad asked.

"It's a bluff," I said. "He's trying to get us to run. But we're safer standing here."

"Isn't there something about playing dead? Should we be playing dead?" Leonard asked.

"No, just keep waving," I said.

The bear closed its jaw and stood still, continuing to look at us with piercing eyes. We looked back, waiting. The bear pounded its two front paws into the dirt, and the ground shook beneath our feet.

"We're okay," I said with a trembling voice.

The bear snorted once. And then again. It put its head to the ground, dug in its claws, and started sprinting toward us at full speed.

Everyone screamed. Leonard and Leo ran into their tent. Dad stood still with his fingers on the tops of the bear spray cans, ready to blast the bear in the face. Laura and I both ducked behind him. I closed my eyes and held Laura's hand tight. The ground was rumbling and I could hear my heart beating in my ears. I braced for impact as time seemed to slow down.

I waited and waited, but nothing happened. The rumbling was over and the forest was quiet.

"He stopped running," Dad whispered to us.

I opened my eyes and peeked around his shoulder. The bear had run forward about fifty feet and was now slowly pivoting to lumber away in the other direction.

"You were right," Dad whispered to me as my heart continued thumping.

"I thought I was dead," Laura said.

I took a deep breath. "We were really lucky," I said.

Dad hugged us close on each side as we watched the black bear continue walking among the trunks of far-off trees.

Leonard unzipped the tent and stuck his head out. "What happened?"

"It was just a bluff," I said. "He wasn't really charging us."

"He was really charging," Laura said.

"But Theo saved us," Dad said.

"Dad protected us," I said.

Leo nudged Leonard aside and stepped out of the tent. "Can you still see it? Can I start filming again?"

"No! Just . . . wait," I said.

As Leo watched despondently, the bear trudged completely out of view.

"There's just one last step," I said. "We need to slowly walk in the other direction a little way. Just to be safe."

I demonstrated, walking away gently without turning my back, and everyone else shuffled after me. Leo turned his phone camera on himself and began narrating a video he later posted with the title "My EPIC ESCAPE from a GNARLY BEAR!"

# EIGHTEEN

**WE RETURNED TO THE CAMPSITE** to quickly clean up. As much as everyone wanted to immediately reminisce about our brush with death, we needed to move out in case the bear returned.

Once we were packed, Dad thrust his hand out for Leonard to shake.

"We've certainly had an exciting time together, but I think it's time for us to part ways," Dad said.

Leonard looked at his hand in shock. "We couldn't possibly split up now," he said. "After all that's happened. Who's to say the bear isn't a member of a larger family?"

Dad looked at me. "He could be right," I said.

"And we'd be so much worse equipped to deal with them in two separate groups than in one larger group, all looking out for each other," Leonard said.

"That *does* make sense," Dad said. "Laura, how do you feel about this?"

"I've already stated my opinion privately and you are well aware of how I feel," Laura said.

"Understood. Theo?" Dad asked.

"I mean, I think we would be safer together. At least for a little while." I wasn't enthusiastic about it, but was willing to endure a few more hours with Leonard and Leo if it increased my chances of surviving the day.

"You see," Leonard said. "The bear expert agrees."

"We're all together, then?" Dad asked.

Laura let out a deep, guttural groan, but yes, we were all together.


While we remained together, we compromised on the direction of the hike. Our journey yesterday left us eight miles from our lodge, and we began the morning on a path that, with a few detours, would eventually lead us back.

We resumed our normal walking order, with Leonard and Dad leading. After saving all our lives, I was deemed cool enough to join Laura and Leo at the back of the pack. But they still didn't want to talk to me very much. Laura kept trying to slow down to indicate that she didn't want to walk next to Leo, but he continuously met her tempo and refused to understand that they weren't playing a game. After several minutes of unsuccessful flirtation along the lines of "surviving something like that brings people closer, huh," he returned to complaining about Leonard.

"Did you see his face when he was running away from the bear?" Leo said.

"Did you see *your* face?" Laura said. "You did the *exact same thing.*"

"Yeah, but he's an adult. He's supposed to take care of me in times of crisis," Leo said. "If my mom was here, we'd already be in the car driving home."

"Our mom was the same," Laura said. "She would never take us on a weeklong camping trip."

"You said she's staying at home?" Leo asked, missing the past tense "was."

"Um . . ." Laura stalled and I knew this stall. I never mentioned Mom unless absolutely necessary and usually lied to strangers so I didn't have to get into it and answer all the follow-up questions.

"Yeah, she's busy. With work," Laura said. "And . . . uh, can't take off as much. Our dad has the summers off, so he can take us on longer trips, but Mom usually stays home."

I picked up the lie. "The whole nature thing is Dad's new hobby. He doesn't really know that much about it."

"Leonard doesn't either," Leo said. "Not really. He started this bird stuff two years ago. Before that he was just, like, a dad. Like a normal person."

"He sounds like he knows what he's doing," I said, having listened to Leonard rattle off the scientific names of birds for hours yesterday.

"He knows birds. But if you weren't here, I don't know if we would have survived that bear."

"Shhh, shhhh, shhhhhh. Listen, listen!" Leonard shouted from the front, waving his arms around to get our attention.

"Here we go," Leo said.

Up ahead, Leonard turned his right ear to the air, craned his neck forward, and froze. I tried to look past him to see what he was listening for, but only saw trees and rocks.

"Are you having a stroke?" Leo asked.

"Listen!" Leonard said insistently.

I could hear the wind, a few birds, and Leo making a fart noise with his mouth.

"I think I can hear it," Dad said.

Leo made another fart noise.

"Stop that!" Leonard hissed.

"Which bird, exactly, are we listening for?" Dad asked.

"It's a very special species," Leonard whispered. "Only found in Texas. Scientific name: *Sitta carolinensis*. Better known as the white-breasted nuthatch."

Leo laughed, then repeated the phrase "white-breasted nuthatch" and cracked himself up again.

"Leonard Jr., we've been over this," Leonard angrily whispered. "The word 'breast' means the protective front of the bird. It has nothing to do with human female breasts. Boobs."

Hearing an angered ornithologist dismissively whisper "boobs" *is* funny, so we all started laughing, which further enraged Leonard.

"It *isn't* funny. White breast. Blue breast. Red breast. These are just classifications."

We continued laughing.

"Stop laughing!" Leonard said. "You're going to scare it away!"

"I haven't even gotten to the nutsack part," Leo said.

"Nut*hatch*."

"That's what I said. The white-breasted nuts hatch."

"White-breasted *nut*hatch. Not *nuts* hatch."

Leo stopped exasperating his father long enough that I could actually hear a distinct birdcall. One that was consistent and stood out from the other noises — like Laura, who was still laughing a little, and Dad, who was rifling through his backpack for binoculars, and Leo, who was checking to see if his phone got service and quietly muttering a curse word.

"That nasal call. The *yonk-yonk-yonk-yonk-ah-ah*," Leonard imitated, "is our guide. I think we just need to go a few more paces."

He slowly led us through a patch of trees.

"Up. Everybody look up," Leonard said as we approached a single gigantic tree. On a bare branch halfway up perched a small white bird. "Do you see it? The white breast. The subtle blue, white, and black interweaving coloration on the feathers. This, my friends, is the white-breasted nuthatch."

"What a beauty," Dad said, adjusting his binoculars.

"A truly one-of-a-kind discovery," Leonard said, pointing his camera in the direction of the rare bird and slowly focusing the lens.

Then, from the back of our group, came a loud, powerful sneeze: "Achhhhhooooooooo!"

It was a sneeze that in such stillness seemed to shake the

trees and chased the precious white-breasted nuthatch away before Leonard could take his coveted picture.

We all spun around to find Laura with her hands covering her face.

"How *dare* you!" Leonard bellowed at her.

She sneezed again.

"Stop that! Right this instant!" Leonard said.

"Don't you mean 'bless you'?" Laura said as she recovered.

"You chased away the white-breasted nuthatch! You don't deserve to be blessed."

"Hey, come on," Dad said. "She didn't do it on purpose."

"Do you have any idea how rare that bird is?" Leonard said. "Only *one* birder found it last year! Do you know how many times it's been photographed this year? *Zero! I* was going to be the first. But then she—"

"*Accidentally* and *uncontrollably* sneezed," Laura said. "Yeah, I'm sorry."

"You don't sound very sorry," Leonard said.

"You just screamed *how dare you* at me. Besides, you saw the bird. Isn't that the point?"

"Yes, I saw it. But it doesn't count if I don't get the picture."

"Well, that seems . . . pretty dumb," she said.

"I think you should both maybe cool off a little," Dad said, stepping between them.

But neither looked like they were going to cool off.

"I don't see what's so *dumb* about wanting to document

the birds you discover throughout the year," Leonard said over Dad's shoulder.

"Couldn't you just enjoy them?" Laura said. "Instead of making it into some big contest."

"Come on, Laura," Dad said.

"Tell *him* to *come on*," Laura said. "All I'm saying is I think it's pretty dumb and honestly kind of offensive that land taken away from Native Americans so that the rest of America could *appreciate nature* is now being used as a competition to see which white man can take the most bird pictures."

"You tell him!" Leo said from the sidelines, phone raised to capture the confrontation.

"Shut up," Laura said. "You're as bad as he is."

"What?" Leo said with a mix of hurt and confusion.

"You don't care about any of this either," Laura said, spreading her arms out to indicate all the nature he didn't care about. "You just want new backgrounds for pictures of yourself so your *fans* don't get bored."

"You can't talk to him like that!" Leonard yelled.

"You can't talk to her like that!" Dad yelled back.

The dads inched toward each other until they stood nearly nose to nose.

"I'm yelling at her because she's yelling at me," Leonard said.

"She's yelling at you because you're yelling at her," Dad said.

"She started it," Leonard said.

"She *sneezed*," Dad said.

Leonard paused and took a step backwards. "Look," he began uncertainly, "we may disagree on some things. But I *do* have a real affinity for birds, photography, and my son. And I will *not* let those things be slandered by some little girl."

"Little girl?!" Laura yelled.

Dad abruptly turned away from Leonard and said, "We're leaving," in the overly calm voice he uses when he's angry. He started walking back in the direction we came and waved his arms for Laura and me to follow.

"Go ahead!" Leonard called.

"We will," Laura called back.

"Just ignore him. Come on," Dad said as he led us through the patch of trees.

"No hard feelings!" Leo called. "The video drops tomorrow!"

Laura deeply exhaled through her nostrils and seemed to use every ounce of her remaining energy to avoid responding. Instead, she said, "Thanks, Dad," as we stepped past the trees and back onto the main path.

# NINETEEN

**LAURA WAS RIGHT.** I think she's usually right. I didn't necessarily think that Leonard symbolized the systematic slaughter of Native Americans by the United States government, but he *was* really annoying. And he shouldn't have screamed at her for sneezing.

However, I didn't think that challenging Leonard at the top of a mountain trail, in one-hundred-plus-degree weather, was the best idea. I had no clue how to make it back to the lodge, doubted she did, and didn't trust Dad's ability to navigate us. He seemed to have stopped paying attention to the trail signs after we joined Leonard and Leo yesterday afternoon. Nevertheless, we kept going down the path before us, hoping it led where we wanted to go.

We made it about two miles before the clouds disappeared and the malicious Texas sun returned. The entire park rippled with heat. Sweat started dripping from my eyelids, and I felt like I would evaporate and join the musty summer air as a particle.

Dad had quickly assumed the Leonard role: pausing, dithering, and noting the things we passed on our journey back to the lodge. Unlike Leonard, he allowed Laura to share her own insights, and the two of them seemed to be enjoying each other's company for the first time in three days. I tried to match their enthusiasm for a while, but there were only so many times that I could half smile and say variations of "oh, wow," "cool," and "I didn't know that." I'd reached my limit after two hours and couldn't appreciate nature for the rest of the day. It was fine. There was great beauty. But I was done.

When we passed a wooden post emblazoned with a yellow picnic table symbol, I begged to stop and eat lunch. Dad wanted to go one more mile before lunchtime, but when I sat down, started wheezing, and said I absolutely could not go one more mile without lunch, he agreed.

I pulled the cooler off my dripping back and set it on the nearest picnic table. As it sat, liquid continued to drip from the bottom of the cooler onto the ground.

"Wait, why is the cooler dripping?" Laura asked.

"Probably because *I'm* dripping and it's been stuck to my back all day," I said, unzipping the top and unleashing the aroma of rotten bananas.

"Just some condensation," Dad added with a smile.

"Or," I said, lifting three warped plastic bags with melted peanut butter smeared around the edges, "maybe because it's broken?"

I plopped the squashed bags of peanut butter goo onto the picnic table and groaned.

"Are you serious?" Laura said, pulling the cooler toward her. She threw three completely black bananas onto the ground and tossed a wet, foggy bag of oranges onto the table.

Dad picked up one of the peanut butter bags and inspected it like a rare artifact. "They might be a little, uh, liquefied, but I think we could still scarf these down."

"Scarf?" I said, picking up a gooey bag. "How am I supposed to *scarf* this?"

"Maybe 'scarf' is the wrong word," Dad said. "But—"

"*Show me* how to *scarf* this?" I said, wagging the bag at Dad.

"Calm down," Laura said. "It's not Dad's fault."

"You're fine with this?" I said to Laura. "Everything else is a problem, but *this* is okay?"

"Why are you getting mad at *me?*" Laura said.

"I'm not mad," I said. "I'm just . . . hungry." But also, I was mad. I'd carried the cooler for two days, saved us from death, and accepted Laura's and Dad's personal indulgences only to be rewarded with a bag of melted food in the middle of a path that might be leading us in the wrong direction.

"I'm sorry this isn't exactly going as planned," Dad said.

"Liquid peanut butter wasn't part of your plan?" I said.

Dad smiled, but I didn't mean it as a joke. "We do need to try to eat these, though," he said. "We're still three miles out and we're going to need some fuel to get us back to the lodge."

He unzipped his warped sandwich bag and started licking out the squished peanut and bread mixture like a dog.

"That's disgusting," I said.

"It's not that bad," Dad said, peanut butter lining his lips. "Go on, dig in."

Left with no other options, I lifted the sandwich bag to my mouth and ate like an animal in the sweltering heat.

"See?" Dad said. "It's still good."

I ignored him, turned to face a tree, and squeezed as much peanut butter as possible into my mouth.

The oppressive heat and lack of proper "fuel" sapped whatever energy Dad and Laura had left. They started saving their words, stopped taking small diversions off the main path, and joined my dedication to getting out of the mountains and into an air-conditioned room as quickly as possible.

The rest of the afternoon passed in silence, sweat, and whatever is the opposite of exhilaration. I was too busy looking ahead, watching the backs of Dad's shoes, to really take in the surroundings. My predominant memory is of heels crushing dirt, with whirring heat fuzzing the edges of my vision.

Just as I feared I would start hallucinating cartoon-style and picture Dad's boots as walking steaks, we staggered onto the paved path that led to our lodge.

"Can you smell that?" Dad said, inhaling dramatically as we approached the front door.

"What?" I said, sniffing to no avail.

"Hot dogs," Dad said. "Bananas . . . that are edible . . ."

"Vegetable-flavored . . . potato sticks . . ." Laura said.

"The *amazing* snacks . . . that Laura bought," Dad said, unlocking the front door.

Laura and I bolted past him to her cache of remaining snacks and started wildly stuffing ourselves. Dad flung his backpack and the broken cooler onto the floor, raced into the kitchen, and ate a banana in two bites.

As we continued throwing pretzels, chips, and gummy worms into our mouths, Dad lined the microwave with six hot dogs and pressed start.

# TWENTY

**LIKE MOST FAMILIES,** as soon as we finished eating, we spread to different corners of the room and turned our attention to our phones. Usually, Dad would at least gently chastise this kind of behavior, but he seemed to have his own texts and emails to catch up on.

With full service, my text to Angel P. finally went through. He quickly replied.

> **ANGEL P.:** omg I thought u were dead. have u heard of battle crash
>
> **ME:** No?
>
> **ANGEL P.:** its a new game everyones playing. get on it. i can send a link.
>
> **ME:** I don't think the service here is good enough to play a game
>
> **ANGEL P.:** oh that sucks. im playing tho so i gotta go. have fun camping!

My "best friend" Angel P. Too busy playing a game that didn't exist a week ago to talk to me for more than a minute. I considered texting Rajneesh, but he's a boring texter. With the recovered use of my earbuds and nothing else to do, I spent the next hour finding and watching Leo's videos. They were deeply stupid and offensive to my sensibilities on a number of levels, but I couldn't stop watching. Maybe it was just the heat exhaustion, but they were transfixing in their awfulness.

My bemused concentration was broken by the loud clap of Dad's hands.

"Family talk!" he said too loudly.

"Pass," Laura said without looking up.

"What?" I said, dazedly dislodging my earbuds.

"Family talk," Dad repeated. "I have some important news to share and I . . . think you, uh, *might* have some questions about it. Even you, Laura."

"We already know the surprise," Laura said, still looking at her phone.

"WHAT?" Dad squawked.

"We went through your stuff," Laura said, putting her phone face-down on the bed. "You rented us two houses for the weekend."

"You *went* through my *stuff,*" Dad said, anger coloring his face.

"For the record, I didn't go through anything," I said. "It was all Laura."

"I wanted to know the surprise," Laura said nonchalantly.

"That doesn't give you the right—" Dad started.

"It's too late now," Laura said.

"Okay. Well . . ." Dad paused and sat down on the bed. "So you found the receipt for the houses. Anything else?"

"We know it's for Craig's birthday," Laura said.

"What?" Dad said with genuine confusion. "Who said anything about Craig?"

"Who else would it be for?" Laura asked.

"I'm going to tell you if you just . . ." Dad said, looking to the floor. "I need you to let me do this the way I want to do this."

"Do *what?*" Laura asked.

He took a deep breath. "Look, I didn't, uh, quite know when to tell you this. I thought I should maybe wait another day, but we were talking and—"

"Who's *we?*" I asked.

Dad laughed nervously. "I, uh, I guess I sort of—"

"So the surprise *is* another person," Laura said.

"Well . . . yes," Dad said.

"Is Grandma coming?" I asked.

"No. Could you maybe—I'm not doing a good job at this. But—" Dad paused. He seemed more nervous than I'd seen him in a long time, possibly ever. "It's . . . a . . . uh, you know . . . a . . . woman."

The air in the room stood still. Laura's jaw dropped. I'm not sure about my own jaw. My mind was whirling but not landing on anything, so it just continued to spin wildly. Several seconds, seemingly minutes, passed in silence.

Finally, Laura said, "So, when you say 'woman,' you mean, like—"

"I had a whole speech prepared," Dad said. "This really is not—I didn't think it would be so . . . dramatic."

"You're not answering the question," Laura said.

"What's the question?" Dad asked.

"Come on," Laura said. "You're going to make me spell it out? Is this person, and this sounds weird even saying out loud, your *girlfriend?*"

The G-word sent another shock through the room. If I were drawing the scene, the word "GIRLFRIEND" would flash in all caps with lightning bolts flaring in every direction. There would be single-panel close-ups of all our eyes in a tense staring match. But in real life, we just sat and stared at each other.

"That's one word for it," Dad said. "Maybe not the best word. We're not technically *dating.*"

"Then what are you doing?" Laura said.

"Just, you know, talking. Isn't that what young people say? 'We're just talking,'" Dad said, doing a bad "young person" impression.

"But you're not a young person," Laura said.

"I'm not *old*. I'm—"

"Okay, never mind," Laura said. "How long have you been *just talking?*"

I didn't know how Laura was able to formulate questions so quickly. I was still too dazed by the fact that Dad had a girlfriend. Or was "just talking" to someone. The whole reveal was so sudden and unexpected that I didn't know how I felt about it.

I had never seriously considered that Dad was single. That there would come a point when he would no longer want to be single. That him not being single would mean he'd have a girlfriend. And that if he really liked that girlfriend, it could mean I'd have a new mom. The whole thing was rapidly piecing itself together in my mind, making it difficult for me to join the discussion.

"A few months," Dad said.

"Few like two or . . . ?" Laura asked.

"Seven or eight months, I guess," Dad said.

*"Seven or eight months?"* Laura said.

"More or less," Dad said.

"How?" Laura said.

"Email," Dad said. "You know, phone calls sometimes."

He *had* been going for late-night walks more regularly over the past few months. Walks that I now knew were just a cover to have long, involved conversations with a secret girlfriend outside of earshot of Laura and me.

"Can you tell us *more?*" Laura pushed. She didn't seem angry but anxious, like her uneasiness would be solved only by knowing everything all at once. "Like, what's her name? How'd you meet?"

"Her name's *Lucrecia*," Dad said, pronouncing it swiftly in an overly precise Spanish accent.

*"Lucrecia?"* Laura squealed.

"What's wrong with *Lucrecia?*" Dad said, again shifting into the proper Spanish pronunciation.

"Nothing's wrong with it," Laura said. "It's just the way you're saying it."

"I'm saying it correctly," Dad said. "Her name's *Lucrecia*."

"Please stop saying it like that," Laura said.

"There's no other way to say it," Dad said.

"Okay, fine," Laura said.

There was a pause. Dad cautiously began, "Anything else you'd like to know, or . . ."

"Um, *who is she?*" Laura asked.

Dad seemed a little calmer now that his secret was out. "She's an old friend. We actually met in college."

"The same college where you met Mom?" Laura asked.

"Yes," he said quietly.

"Did Mom *know her?*" Laura asked pointedly.

"Um . . . somewhat," he said. "We were all sort of in the same . . . friend group."

"Were they, like, good friends?" Laura asked.

"I wouldn't say that. More acquaintances than friends, I guess."

Laura paused for a minute to think. "Do you promise that you're not dating one of Mom's old friends?"

Dad looked down and then directly into Laura's eyes. "Yes. I promise. And we're not dating. Like I said, we're just talking."

"But she's coming here, right?" I said, finally finding an entry point into the conversation. "If she's joining our vacation, then you're dating."

"This is more of a test," Dad said.

"I don't like tests," I said.

"'Test' isn't the right word," Dad said. "I want to see how everyone gets along. To see if you like her. Like a trial run. Is that a better way to say it?"

"Not really," I said. "That makes it sound like we're being used in an experiment."

"Well, this is kind of an experiment," Dad said. "And it can be a fun experiment or it can be an awful experiment. I think it kind of depends on how you treat her."

"It depends on how she treats us first," Laura said.

"She's going to treat you like the kind and caring person that she is."

"Ew," Laura said, scrunching up her face.

"You wanted to know what she's like," Dad said, his voice rising above the calm-Dad tone he'd been trying to stick to.

"I want to know *who* she is," Laura said. "Like, what's her job. Not why you like her."

"She's a life coach," Dad said.

"What's a life coach?" Laura asked.

"It's someone who helps other people become better versions of themselves," Dad said.

"Like a therapist?" Laura asked.

"Not exactly," Dad said. "It's more like someone who helps people achieve their goals."

"That sounds like therapy," Laura said.

"You can call it therapy if you have to," Dad said.

"So you're dating your therapist," Laura said.

"No," Dad said, his face reddening, "I was just trying to clarify. I don't have a therapist. And she's not *my* life coach. She's *a* life coach."

"But she's helping you to achieve your goals," Laura said.

"Well, yes, kind of," Dad said.

"So she's your life coach," Laura said.

"This is very frustrating," Dad said.

"I'm kidding," Laura said.

"She's my old friend. She's a life coach. We reconnected a few months ago. She's been a big help to me. Okay? Anything else?"

"I'm still processing all of this," Laura said.

"Theo?" Dad asked.

I still didn't know how I felt about it. I guess I was okay. I mean, it didn't really matter. He'd already made up his mind to invite her on our trip. Even if I weren't okay with it, she'd still be here the day after tomorrow. This was another one of Dad's questions that wasn't actually a question. "She sounds . . . good," I said.

"Well, she is . . . good," Dad said, mocking my response in a way that made me angry. "And I hope you'll both be nice to her."

"We'll see," Laura said.

"No promises," I said.

# TWENTY-ONE

**THE NEXT MORNING** was the Fourth of July, and Dad was up early talking about the glory of the United States. He said that we should also focus on celebrating our country's many wonderful qualities instead of fixating on the fact that he'd been hiding a secret girlfriend for seven months.

Laura argued that while America certainly has *some* good qualities, it was also a country founded on Native American land that shipped in slaves and didn't let women own property or vote until the twentieth century. Dad quickly changed the subject to fireworks. I said fireworks are boring and if you've seen them once, you've seen them all. Dad disagreed and started recounting his favorite fireworks experiences until we begged him to stop.

Irritated by our indifference toward the wondrousness of America and fireworks, Dad decided to walk to the Visitor Center for breakfast. As soon as he left, Laura immediately fell back asleep. I tried to sleep too, but her persistent snoring prevented me from ever fully drifting off. After a few minutes, I gave up and instead took out my notebook.

I flipped through the first nine pages of *Bob: The Boy with Perfect Memory,* convinced it was the best work I had ever done. I was still at the part where Bob decides to take the pill that would turn him into Bob: The Boy with Normal Memory. I drew the scientist explaining the process. First, the scientist says, he will demonstrate how the pill works. He hooks Bob up to a machine that projects all his memories onto a big screen.

Think of the happiest days of your life, the scientist instructs Bob.

I drew three panels to represent the happiest days of Bob's life. In the first panel is the day he turned five, when his mom threw him a surprise birthday party in the backyard with special guest SpongeBob SquarePants.

In the second panel is the day his mom picked him up early from school and took him to an R-rated movie. I drew Bob and his mom laughing in their seats as popcorn spilled into their laps.

While I tried to think of what to draw in the third panel, Laura's snoring intensified. It became so distracting that I set my notebook aside and moved on to the next best thing: plugging in my phone and searching for Lucrecia on all existing social media platforms.

I started with Dad's Facebook because that's how old people interact online. Since he has only 183 friends, it was an easy hunt down to *L*, and *Lu*, and then there she was: Lucrecia Zampano. I opened another tab to search for the meaning of the last name Zampano. One site said it was Italian for "chief" or "leader." Another said it was German and translated to "the big cheese." Lucrecia "the Big Cheese" Zampano and Stanley "Dad" Ripley.

I went back to the Facebook tab and clicked on her profile. It was entirely private besides one profile picture where she's wearing a plain but fashionable black sweater and somewhat smiling. From her single viewable picture, she seemed like one of those older yoga women who post pictures of smoothies, vegetables, and their own pools.

I switched over to Instagram to verify my assumptions. Dad doesn't have an account, so I had to search her name and hope she showed up. Of the four Lucrecia Zampanos with viewable accounts, two seemed too young, and one too old. The only real possibility was a woman whose feed featured 40 percent pictures of plants and 60 percent pictures of cats. Hopefully, this was not the Big Cheese.

"I just had the craziest dreams," Laura said. I was so absorbed in my sleuthing that I hadn't registered that Laura's snoring had stopped. "Do you want to hear about them?"

"No," I said, still scrolling through plants to try to find a picture of a face.

"Can I tell you at least one? You were in it . . ."

I turned and set my phone on the bedside table. "Okay. But make it short. As short as possible. Under one minute."

"I can make it short!" Laura said, sliding up into a sitting position to narrate her meaningless dream.

I said nothing but stared at her with dead eyes, which she hates. I kept boring my dead eyes in her direction until she said, "Seriously, stop."

I didn't stop, even though I was getting a minor headache.

Slight feelings of discomfort are acceptable to prevent your sister from describing her dreams.

"I get it. You can stop."

Victorious, I stopped.

Laura immediately jumped into her dream. "So I was at home and a bird came to my window. It was a black bird, but not a blackbird, it was more—"

"Do you want to see a picture of Lucrecia!" I shouted.

"What?" Through the morning haze, it took her a few seconds to register the words I'd used to shut her up. Slowly, the meaning clicked and she beamed. "Yes! Duh. Where?"

"Here," I said, passing my phone over to her outstretched hand.

She brought the screen close to her face. Then held it farther away and started fiddling, tilting the screen and adjusting the brightness.

"Well?" I prompted.

She handed my phone back, done examining the one available picture from every possible angle. "She's pretty. Not that that matters, but she is. Honestly, she's much better-looking than Dad. What do you think?"

"Yeah, I mean, she's all right," I said, not wanting to get into a detailed discussion about the looks of Dad's new girlfriend at 9:00 a.m.

"Did you find anything else?" Laura asked, now using her phone to conduct her own investigation.

"Um, not really. Her last name is Zampano, which means 'the big cheese' in German."

"I don't really think that's important. Did you see this?" Laura said, rapidly typing and scrolling. "Reviews for her life coaching company."

"I hadn't gotten that far. What's it called?"

"Lucrecia Zampano Coaching," Laura said. "Listen to this one—'Five stars. Working with Lucrecia helped me to take my life to the next level. She responded to my highs and lows and helped to untangle all of the fears that limit my belief in myself.'"

"Whoa," I said, half listening while scrolling, "did you see this one? It's one star and the person complains that she's too pushy."

"Yeah, there's some bad ones. But they're mostly pretty good. Here's another five stars. Listen to this one—"

As she took a breath to start reading, the distinct sound of jostling keys rang from outside the door. Laura started frantically swiping to close every open tab on her phone. I did the same as Dad quietly crept into the room.

Noticing that we were both fully awake, he stopped trying to sneak around and looked at us like a detective, seeming to sense something suspicious in the air. "What are you all up to?"

"Nothing," Laura said.

"Just hanging out, normal-style," I said.

We both sheepishly smiled from our beds.

"Okay," he said, still looking suspicious. "I'm going to take a shower and let you get back to your normal hanging out in here."

"Great idea. I wasn't going to say anything but you seriously smell," Laura said.

"I don't smell *that* bad, do I?" Dad asked, raising his armpit to his nose.

"Yes," Laura said.

"You should have showered last night," I said.

"Okay, okay. I'm going," he said.

As soon as he gathered his things and headed for the small bathroom, my phone buzzed.

**LAURA:** this is the review I was going to read. it's even better than the last one.

I looked over at Laura. "Do we have to text?" I asked out loud.

She bugged her eyes out, motioned for me to start typing, and silently mouthed, "Yes."

I rolled my eyes and began texting her from five feet away.

**ME:** I already read it. She sounds like she's good at her job. Probably also a good person.

**LAURA:** I think so too but then why is she single?

**ME:** Maybe she's divorced like most people.

**LAURA:** Yeah, but why?

**ME:** I don't know. Why don't you ask Dad?

**LAURA:** Yeah right

**ME:** Then wait until tomorrow and ask her.

**LAURA:** I can't ask her that

**ME:** I can't help you.

**LAURA:** 💀

# TWENTY-TWO

**WHEN DAD GOT OUT** of the shower, he announced that today would be a treat day. He didn't say it in those words, exactly, but he used phrases like "whatever you want," "this day is completely up to you two," and "I am at your command," which indicated that today was going to be a treat day.

I knew that he was trying to trick us. That he wanted to make up for getting lost in Leonard's bird fantasia, and for the broken cooler, and for revealing his secret girlfriend way later than he should have. That he was just trying to change the momentum heading into our big weekend with the Big Cheese. But Laura and I also didn't want to waste the opportunity to plan a fun day, so we huddled over the one table to map out the itinerary.

She thumbed through her detailed Big Bend notebook. I said I'd go along with whatever she wanted to do as long as we were indoors, riding in a car, or eating for 80 percent of the day. She said that seemed like kind of a waste of a day. I said she seemed like kind of a waste of a day. We continued along this line of discussion before eventually settling on a plan that was 60 percent inside and 40 percent outside.

It began with the Ross Maxwell Scenic Drive, a looping

thirty-mile paved trail that winds through the parts of the park difficult to reach by foot. Dad made us agree to not bring up Lucrecia during the drive. This was going to be the last chance for us to experience the park together, and we should enjoy it, rather than asking him more questions about his mysterious girlfriend, who we'd meet tomorrow.

Laura said she would agree to his terms if it meant she could ask questions about Lucrecia in the afternoon. Dad reluctantly accepted this counteroffer. While it was difficult to completely turn off my brain from wondering what would come tomorrow, I was happy to have some relief from Laura and Dad's consistent squabbling, and also agreed.

With everyone in agreement, a sense of temporary peace permeated the car. Dad asked Laura non-condescending questions about land formations and she answered them sincerely, happy to finally have her research appreciated and her daily plan followed. His dedication to mispronouncing "butte" as "butt" at every opportunity was excused with a mild eye roll and never devolved into an argument.

I was relaxing in the back seat, enjoying the ability to experience nature through the windows of an air-conditioned vehicle, which is how I like to be in touch with nature. By not touching it, just viewing it.

The scenic drive ended at the famous (to Laura) Boquillas Hot Springs.

"Is this it?" Dad asked when our car reached the last strip of pavement.

"Does the sign say 'Boquillas Hot Springs'?" Laura said.

"It says 'Boquillas Hot Springs: one point one miles,'" Dad said.

"Then yes," Laura said. "We have to walk one point one miles. I didn't mention that part."

At least it was an easy path, one that took us only twenty minutes before we heard running water and voices speaking loudly in another language. We rounded the last corner and came to a large brown sign that read:

## HOT SPRINGS RULES
Be respectful of others
Bathing suits are recommended
Swimming underwater is not recommended
Alcoholic beverages are prohibited

Just beyond the sign was a blue-gray river and a dark blue rectangular pool blocked off by heavy stone slabs. Inside the unbelievably blue rectangle were the foreign speakers in the flesh. By "in the flesh" I mean they were naked. I knew they were naked because I could see the woman's breasts. It was an older woman, probably in her sixties, so it was more surprising than exciting. They, the breasts, were slumped over the water, resting on the surface of the hot springs like lily pads. Thankfully, everything else was covered by the dark blue water.

Laura and Dad were still reading the rules.

"Um, Dad, I think they're naked," I said. "And drinking." Next to the elderly couple were two bottles of wine and two plastic cups, half-filled.

"Wait, what?" Laura exclaimed, darting her head around the sign.

"Bonjour!" called the naked grandma.

"Hiii!" Laura yelled to her before whispering to us, "Yeah, she's not wearing clothes."

"Why can't people just follow the rules?" Dad said, flailing his arms at the sign.

"Technically, bathing suits are just recommended," I said.

"But before that it says be respectful of others," Dad said.

"There weren't any others before we got here," I said. "So they weren't *dis*respecting anyone."

"Do you want to get in there with them?" Dad asked.

"Not really," I said.

"Definitely not," Laura said.

"Bonjour! Hello!" the woman called out again.

"Wait here," Dad said to us before stepping out from behind the sign and walking toward the couple.

"Hello," he said warmly.

"Nice to see you," the woman said in heavily accented English. "I see your children, they are, ah, peeking."

Dad turned around and gestured for us to get behind the sign. We did. Then he turned around and we stuck our heads back out to watch what would happen next.

"About them," Dad said, now standing a few paces away from the hot springs. "I would like to talk to you about my children, if you don't mind."

"Yes, it is okay. They can come into the water. It will not bother us. This is Bernard," she said, indicating the old man next to her. "His English is not, ah, strong."

"Hello," he said, holding up his plastic cup of wine in salute.

"You are from . . . France?" Dad asked.

"Oui, yes," she said. "We are from Nor-man-dee. I am Sylvie."

"Sylvie. Bernard. It's nice to meet you. It looks like you're having a good time." Dad paused and put on his more serious voice. "But I think you may have missed the rules for this area." He pointed toward the sign. "It says that you need to wear bathing suits. Here, in this water. So that's one thing. And it also says you can't drink alcohol."

"Oh yes," she said. "We saw these. But I think these, the rules here, they are silly."

"Silly?" Dad asked.

"Silly, yes. We come here to nature to be free. To enjoy. These rules, to us, they are not good."

"Well, that's one way of looking at it," Dad said. "I, however, have two children, who you saw."

"Yes, I see them. They are still peeking."

Dad turned around and mouthed, "I said *wait*."

We shrugged and continued watching.

Slowly, he turned back around to face the nude French couple, exhaling deeply.

"They are no bother," Sylvie said. "They can come into the water. It is hot and good."

"I'm happy you feel that way, but *they* are the ones who are bothered. They are bothered by your, uh, lack of clothing."

"Lack of clothing?" she questioned.

"You're . . ." He spun his hands around, searching for a better phrase, but came up with "Naked. Nude. Not wearing clothes."

"Ah, yes," she said, looking down. "It is a problem?"

"Yes. For them, it is a problem."

"But it is the human body. What is the problem to be human and have a body?"

"Being human and having a body is not the problem. It's, uh, not covering the body in public that's the problem."

"If I want to take my body out of my clothes, it is for me to decide. I have this right."

"Yes, that's true. But the *rules* say that bathing suits are recommended."

"Recommend means it is not the law, no?"

"Yes, technically, that's true."

"Then I do not need this bath suit."

"But the rules *do* say that drinking is *prohibited*. That means one hundred percent not allowed. It certainly looks like you're both drinking."

"As I say, these rules are silly."

"I could get a park ranger who doesn't think they're silly," Dad threatened.

"A tough man, eh? You are going to be a tough man?"

"I'm not trying to be a tough man."

"It sounds like you are, tough man."

"Stop calling me tough man. I just want my kids to be able to get into some warm water without seeing two naked people. Is that so much to ask?"

She paused and started speaking with Bernard in French. They spoke for a minute before she translated for Dad. "Bernard says he will not put on his shorts. He is being free."

Dad was on the verge of yelling. "You tell Bernard that . . . never mind. Look, if I gave you twenty dollars, would you please put something on?"

Sylvie translated for Bernard again. "We will take the money, tough man," she said.

# TWENTY-THREE

**AS SYLVIE AND BERNARD** nakedly stumbled back to their car to get dressed, we moved our bathing-suited bodies down to the hot springs. If I'd paid better attention to Laura this morning, I'd have known that the hot springs were going to be more of an endurance test than a relaxing time. The water stayed at a constant 105 degrees and as soon as I stepped in, I started boiling.

After five minutes, I was woozy and couldn't think straight. Laura said this was the purpose of hot springs in some cultures. If I allowed it, the boiling water would unharness my mind from its usual patterns of thinking. But I didn't want to take a spiritual journey into higher consciousness. I wanted to take a warm, relaxing bath and maybe swim around a little without putting my head underwater.

Fortunately, if you climb over the hot springs' rocks, you land directly in the comparatively ice-cold water of the Rio Grande. While I had to remain alert and keep ahold of the rocks to prevent the river's flow from dragging me away, the rushing tide of the Rio Grande cooled me into a normal, enjoyable mental state.

But I was the only one who hopped out. Despite sweating

profusely, Dad claimed that he had entered a state of bliss. Laura was completely red from head to foot but stayed in to protect her pride, I guess. She wouldn't admit that coming to a hot spring in July was a bad idea.

As Dad continued praising the healing powers of the water, Sylvie and Bernard came tottering back down in their underwear.

"This is okay for you? We do not have a bath suit," Sylvie called.

"It'll do," Dad said. "Thank you for changing."

"You are sure your children, they are not bothered?" she asked, carefully stepping over the rocks and re-situating herself next to the two bottles of wine. Bernard, in shiningly bright tighty-whitey underwear and dark sunglasses, got in next to her. They took turns pouring more wine into their plastic cups as Laura and I introduced ourselves.

Bernard started speaking in French. Sylvie translated: "He says he had a friend from childhood called Theo."

Bernard kept talking animatedly, occasionally pausing for Sylvie to translate.

"He says that Theo was—I do not know the best word—playboy?" Pause. "He liked many women." Pause. "One of the women was the sister of Bernard." Pause. "She was a great beauty." Pause. "The men in the town said the sister of Bernard had the most beautiful backside. Is 'backside' correct? Her buttocks."

"Can I stop you there?" Dad cut in.

I looked at Laura and we both started laughing. I was laughing so hard I nearly lost my hold on the rocks.

"Bernard says there is more to the story," Sylvie said.

"I'm sure there is," Dad said.

"Your children are enjoying it. Laughing. Having a nice time."

"They're having a nice time, but I think the story may be going somewhere we'd rather not go."

"It is good to talk to children about love, no?" Sylvie said, and took another long sip of wine.

"We may have different parenting philosophies," Dad said.

"When I was your daughter's age, I was already breaking many hearts," Sylvie said. "Have you done this, breaking hearts?" she asked Laura.

"You don't have to answer that," Dad said.

"I want to," Laura said. "But no. I don't think I've broken any hearts."

"It is a shame, but you are still young." She turned her attention to me. "How about you? You have been in love?"

"Um . . . no," I said.

"How about a kiss?" she asked. "You have given a kiss?"

I eyed Dad, who looked like he wanted to be anywhere else.

"No," I said. "I've never kissed anyone." Sad but true.

"You have kissed?" she asked Laura.

"Yes," Laura said shyly.

"What?!" Dad and I both shouted in astonishment.

"It is good for a young woman to kiss many different men," Sylvie said.

I asked, "Who was it?"

Dad asked, "Have you kissed *many men?*"

"Just . . . one," Laura said. "But I'm not telling."

I said, "You can't say you've kissed someone and not tell us who it is."

"You should at least tell me," Dad said. "I need to make sure—"

Sylvie cut him off. "A woman can have her secrets. She does not need to name her lover."

"Lover?" Dad said with wide eyes.

"Just a kiss," Laura said.

Bernard spoke in French and Sylvie translated. "He says if he was a young man, he would give a kiss to Laura."

"Ewww!" Laura said.

"You tell Bernard to settle down," Dad said.

Bernard laughed.

"You still haven't answered the question," I said. "Who was it?"

"I'm not telling you!" Laura said.

"See, it is good to talk of love," Sylvie said. "You have a kissing daughter. Soon you have a kissing son. This is the way it should be. No shame."

#  TWENTY-FOUR

**THERE WAS SHAME, THOUGH,** because we weren't the kind of family that talked about kissing, or love, or death, or pain, or anything like that. But Sylvie and Bernard had started the conversation and Dad, perhaps mentally warped by the sun or just trying to fill the quiet of the car ride back to the lodge, continued it.

"You know, Laura, you *can* talk to me about your love life," he said.

"Oh my god," Laura said, covering her face with her hands.

"I'm being serious," Dad continued. "You can tell me things."

"*Please* stop," she said. "I'm not doing this."

"You know, you can always talk to *me* about your love life," I said.

Laura turned and punched me in the shoulder.

"No fighting!" Dad shouted before immediately lowering his voice. "I'm sorry. I didn't mean to yell. But I *am* being serious. We can talk about these things if you want to."

"Since when?" Laura said. "You never want to talk about anything important."

"Maybe that was true in the past," Dad said. "But I'm trying to change. To be more open. To, you know, grow."

"Because of your *new girlfriend?*" Laura said.

"Maybe," Dad said uncertainly.

"That means we can actually talk about her now?" Laura asked.

Dad sighed. "Could we maybe wait until we're back at the lodge?"

"No," Laura said. "You agreed that we could ask questions after noon. It's way after noon."

"Do you really have more questions?" Dad said. "I remember answering a lot of questions last night."

"We were in shock," Laura said. "I couldn't think of the really *important* questions. Theo has questions too—he just isn't saying anything."

"You have questions, Theo?" Dad asked.

"I mean, yeah, obviously, but we don't need to do this right now if you don't want to," I said.

"Stop being a baby," Laura said.

"Don't call him a baby," Dad said.

"But he's *being* a baby. *Acting* like a baby," Laura said.

"I'm not being a baby," I said. "You're the one being a . . . word that starts with *b*."

"I don't like that kind of language," Dad said.

"That's not what I was going to say," I said. "I was going to call her another B-word."

"Uh-huh, what B-word?" she said.

"Butthole," I said.

"Dad!" she yelled.

"Theo! Apologize to your sister," Dad said.

"Laura," I said, taking her hand and looking into her eyes, "I apologize for calling you a butthole."

She flicked my knuckle incredibly hard.

"Ow!" I yelled. "Make *her* apologize."

"Cool it! Both of you!" Dad said. "Do I need to pull over?" He peered into the rearview mirror and carefully inspected our faces.

"No," we both said angrily.

"All right," Dad said, letting the tension cool for several seconds. "Now, if you have some questions about . . . Lucrecia," he said, his voice nearly trembling, "I'll answer them."

Laura started digging through her backpack. "Great! I wrote some down."

"You wrote questions *down?*" Dad said.

"I wanted to organize my thoughts," Laura said.

"Oh boy," Dad said. "Do you have any . . . easier questions, Theo?"

Of course I had questions. I wanted to know how long they were actually "just talking." Exactly how long after Mom's death he felt like he needed someone to "just talk" to. Why he couldn't spend more time talking to us instead of finding someone else to talk to. Why he felt like it was okay to go on long walks every night and come back smiling and never explain himself. Why whenever I asked him what he was smiling about he would just shrug and say he was listening to a funny podcast. Why he thought it was completely fine to lie and lie and lie and then expect us to be excited.

Why he believed that we would think spending time with his new girlfriend was some special treat.

But I didn't have my thoughts organized like Laura. I didn't know how to put them together one by one and figured they would just come out as a long, confusing question that wasn't really a question, so I just said, "I want to hear Laura's questions first."

"Question one," Laura said, having found her page—or, it looked like, pages—of questions. "What have you told her about us?"

"Okay," Dad said. He was noticeably tense, his shoulders hunched, his eyes stuck firmly ahead on the road. But he'd asked for it. "I don't know. I told her that you're fifteen and thirteen. That I love you both very much. Um, that Theo can be kind of quiet."

"I'm not quiet," I said. "Laura's just always talking."

"Shut up," Laura said.

"See," I said. "She's silencing me."

"Does that answer your question?" Dad said, hoping to be let off the hook.

"No. What did you say about me?" Laura pressed.

"That you're not as quiet. But very smart. And—"

"You didn't say that *I'm* smart?" I said.

"I said you were both very smart," Dad said. "What's the next question?"

"That's not a good answer, but okay," Laura said. "Question two: Why is she single?"

Dad sighed. "She's divorced."

"Why?" Laura asked.

"I don't know. People get divorced."

"But why did *she* get divorced?"

"You'll have to ask her."

"That wouldn't be polite."

"You don't get to know everything you'd like to know."

"But I'd prefer to."

"Tough luck. Question three?"

"You realize," Laura said, "that you're not actually being very open."

"I'm trying my best. What's the next question?"

"You have to be open for this one," Laura said.

"I'm open, come on," Dad said, growing impatient.

"Okay, question three," Laura said. "What's the likelihood that you'll get married?"

Dad said nothing but stared at Laura in the rearview mirror. Several seconds passed before he mumbled, "I don't know."

"That's not an answer," Laura said.

"How am I supposed to know?" Dad said. "You've never met her, and she's never met you. Those are important steps that we all have to take before I would even think about something like getting married."

"But what's the *likelihood*?" Laura pushed. "A percentage, maybe?"

Ahead of us, the sky lit up with exploding fireworks.

"Well, look at that!" Dad exclaimed. "Those are some real beauties. They must be a couple of miles ahead."

"You haven't answered the question," Laura said.

"Do you want to go watch the fireworks?" Dad asked.

"No," I said.

"Obviously not," Laura said.

"Come on. Let's go have a look," Dad said, steering our car toward the flashing lights, evading Laura's questions and ignoring our indifference toward booming explosions in the sky. He never answered the last question.

# TWENTY-FIVE

**THE NEXT MORNING,** Dad woke us up at 8:00 a.m. It was the big day and he was noticeably antsy. While he was wearing a blue tie-dye shirt that said GRATEFUL DAD, he strongly suggested that we wear something "presentable," since "there's no impression like the first impression." I had three shirts left at the bottom of my backpack and put on the least wrinkled.

Presentable and packed, we headed toward the two small houses in the desert. While I knew what they looked like from the printout, I didn't know anything about the town they sat in. Dad said that because we'd already ruined the surprise, he wouldn't tell us anything further until we arrived.

Forty minutes later, he turned onto a dirt road marked with a small sign: TERLINGUA GHOST TOWN, POPULATION 58. I objected to spending the weekend in a town designed for ghosts, but Dad clarified that "ghost town" is an old phrase for a town that's been abandoned over time. That made more sense, because I can't imagine ghosts wanting to live in a town filled with trailer parks, small restaurants, and rolling tumbleweeds.

As we continued down the dirt road at a crawl, the sights became weirder. Between the trailer parks and restaurants were huge pieces of art—a dinosaur made of wire, a ten-foot lizard

136

made of glass, a multicolored dome — and fake tepees that were either art installations or offensive hotels.

When we came to a large adobe house with a PSYCHIC: PALM AND CARD READINGS sign perched in the window, Dad turned right onto a narrow, rocky path that led to the two houses from the printout.

We unloaded the car and made our way to the front porch, where a rainbow-colored tie-dye sheet fluttered from a short flagpole.

"This is actually cool, maybe," Laura said. "From outward appearances."

"It's plenty cool on the inside, too," Dad said while waving the dumbest hang-ten hand gesture I've ever seen.

"That means there's air conditioning?" I asked.

"I'm pretty sure," he said, taking the key from a porch table and unlocking the front door.

The door opened into the kitchen, where there was, thankfully, an air conditioning vent. Past the kitchen was a room with two beds and a ladder leading up to a loft area with a futon cushion on a rug. Laura immediately claimed this space as her own.

"Then *this* is your corner," Dad told me, indicating the bed and nightstand next to the window. "And this door" — he opened a rickety screen door — "leads to our outdoor bathroom. Which, if you'll excuse me, I'm going to try out."

He walked out with his suitcase to the small square box a few steps from the door.

"I happen to like this place," Laura said as she climbed down from her loft.

"Did you see the outdoor bathroom?" I asked. "Dad's breaking it in with a big dump right now."

"Why are you like this?" she said.

I shrugged and lay down on my new bed. Laura shuffled the stack of brochures and maps lying on the nightstand.

"What are we doing today?" I asked her.

"I don't know. This is Dad's big *surprise*. I didn't look up what to do in a ghost town." She sat down on the bed next to me and began leafing through the brochures. "This says the 'heart' of Terlingua is their seven restaurants. We could eat a lot, I guess." She picked up another brochure. "But the best restaurant is called Eddie's Edible Tex Mex, so—"

She was disrupted by the creaking of the door as Dad gingerly stepped back into the room. An aroma of potent cologne filled the air. In four minutes, Dad had transformed into a different person. He'd gelled his hair into a style that was meant to be fashionable and was wearing a tighter-than-I-had-ever-seen-him-wear-before navy polo shirt and tighter-than-I-had-ever-seen-him-wear-before gray jogging pants that stopped above his ankles. On his feet were spotless white tennis shoes.

To someone who hadn't seen him dress in the exact opposite way for thirteen years, he may have looked normal. To me, however, he looked ridiculous. Like a man who saw one fashion magazine and bought the outfit on the cover.

"Oh my god," Laura said. "*Who* is this? *What* is this?"

"I don't want to hear it," Dad said, resolutely setting his things down next to the bed and avoiding eye contact.

"You can't walk in here dressed like that and expect us to not ask twenty questions," Laura said. "What do you call this look?"

"I can look *nice* if I want to," Dad said begrudgingly.

"Is this fashion advice from good parents dot com?" Laura asked.

"No," he said.

"Cool dads dot gov?" I suggested.

There was a sharp knock at the front door. Dad was momentarily saved from our mocking as all eyes turned toward the window. Could this be the Big Cheese herself? I felt an impulsive flurry in my chest, the same kind of hyper-charged anxiety and lightheadedness I feel before I have to present something at school. Dad swung open the door while Laura and I peeked from the shadows of the other room.

It was a tiny elderly woman dressed in all white. Definitely not Lucrecia.

"Howdy. You must be Mr. Ripley," she said, extending her hand toward Dad. "Celeste. Welcome. I just saw you pull in and wanted to give you some information about the property. Everything should be in working order. The art you see on the walls? It's mine and for sale, if interested."

My eyes had drifted past them before, but hanging on the kitchen walls were seven framed paintings of cacti performing human activities. My favorite was a fat cactus robbing a bank.

"Very impressive," Dad said, scanning the walls to find something to compliment. "I like this one, with the baby cactus changing a tire."

"Oh yes, that's one of my favorites too," she said, beaming. "It's on sale for four hundred dollars if you'd be interested in purchasing."

"I'll think about it," Dad said.

"You do that. Think it over," she said, smiling. "Other things to know: You probably saw the sign out front. At any time, I'm also available for palm or tarot card readings. Just let me know."

"We'll let you know," Dad said, smiling.

"You're interested in a reading?" she asked.

"We'll have to see," Dad said, politely hinting for her to leave her own rented porch. As Dad smiled and waited for the lingering psychic to get the hint, another car slowly crunched into view.

The psychic turned and said, "That must be your other guest. I knew she'd pull up soon. That's why I came over here. I sensed a great anticipation and wanted to be here to experience it firsthand."

Dad squinted to see the driver of the approaching car. His smile turned from strained to excited. "Yes, that's her. We're all very excited to see her."

"I don't sense excitement from everyone," the psychic said.

"*I'm* very excited," Dad said.

"We'll see how long that lasts," she said.

"What was that?" Dad said, half listening while waving to Lucrecia.

"Nothing," she said. "Enjoy your stay." She turned and slowly walked the dusty path back to her corner house.

Dad zipped out to Lucrecia's expensive-looking car as Laura and I moved to peer out the kitchen window.

"Do you think they're going to kiss?" I said.

"Eww. Why would you say that?" Laura said.

"I don't want to watch them kiss."

"Just shut up. I want to hear what they're saying."

We watched as Lucrecia got out of the car. She was wearing sunglasses, a gray T-shirt, olive pants, and hiking boots. She was better-looking than her profile picture. For sure, she was better-looking than Dad.

Dad, perhaps sensing that we were watching, lightly patted her on the back but didn't go in for a hug or kiss. They were far enough away that we couldn't hear what they were whispering to each other.

"What do you think?" Laura asked.

"I don't know. What do you think?" I said.

"I don't really know how to describe it, but it feels weird," she said.

"I know what you mean," I said.

"Like my stomach feels unsettled."

"Dad looks really stupid. I think that's part of it."

"They do kind of match, though," Laura said. "I can see why he changed."

"He still looks stupid," I said.

They turned and, holding hands, headed toward the front door.

"Act normal," Laura said.

"You act normal," I said.

# TWENTY-SIX

**WE PRETENDED TO BE** casually checking our phones at the kitchen table when the front door opened.

"This. Is. Lucrecia!" Dad said in an excitedly high-pitched voice, presenting her like a game-show host unveiling a new car.

"Hiiii!" she said, setting two gift bags on the counter and rushing toward us with open arms. "It's so wonderful to meet you. I'm a hugger."

We were not huggers, so it was slightly awkward when she squeezed our upper bodies before we could get up. I kind of half stood up as she was hugging me but then quickly sat back down.

"Thank you," I mumbled.

"What was that?" she asked.

"Oh, nothing. I was saying thank you. For the hug," I said. I didn't know why I was talking or what I was saying, and I wished I could disappear.

"Of course," she said, resuming her position next to Dad, their shoulders comfortably touching. I couldn't see exactly, but it looked like he was gently rubbing her back. The whole touching situation was already way beyond what I expected or wanted to experience.

"It really is a pleasure to meet both of you. Your father has told me so much about you," she said with a bright smile, turning toward Dad, who was smiling reassuringly, and then back toward Laura and me, who were smiling nervously.

For several seconds we all looked at one another with different smiles on our faces, waiting for someone to say something.

"Well," Lucrecia began, thankfully ending the smiling contest, "I also brought you each a little something." She picked up the two bags from the counter. "I know it may sound a little cheesy, but I feel that you've already given *me* such a gift by allowing me to join your vacation. The least I can do is give you something in return." She set down the two personalized gift bags on the table in front of us.

"Well, how about that!" Dad said in the voice he used when we were young children unimpressed by a clown.

But I was impressed. I certainly wasn't going to turn down a free present. "Thank you," I said graciously.

Laura seemed less enthused. "Thanks," she said sullenly.

"You can open them if you'd like," Lucrecia said.

I quickly tossed the tissue paper aside and pulled out a thick black notebook with my initials, TR, stamped on the bottom right corner.

"I did my best to tailor them to your interests," Lucrecia said. "Your father said that you like drawing comics, Theo. So if you actually open that, you'll see that each page is already a series of panels, so you don't even have to worry about making rectangles before filling them in. I thought it would maybe save you some time or help to spark some ideas. Not that I've seen your drawing or know how you like to draw, but I'd like to, if you want to share."

I tried to squeeze in another thank-you but she had turned her attention to Laura, who was carefully unwrapping a book titled *Tales of the Big Bend*. "You were much harder to shop for, Laura. Your father said your main interest was proving him wrong. Which was maybe a joke, and maybe something I shouldn't be telling you, but with a little more *prying* he revealed your interest in local history. That book is, by most accounts, the best historical record of this area. I hope you like it."

We both thanked her and waited for Dad to say something, to direct us in some way toward what was happening next. He didn't and instead continued smiling, glanced around the room, and lightly bobbed his head.

After a few more seconds of strained silence, Lucrecia said, "Well, I'm going to go get settled next door. I've heard Laura's the planner here, but I do have some suggestions of my own for today only, if you don't mind?"

"Sure," Laura said. "I don't have anything planned for today."

"Great! Again, so nice to meet both of you. I think we can have a really *fun* time together, if you'd like to." She looked at us and flashed another large smile before turning and walking out the front door. Dad followed and led her into her own house next door. Laura and I waited until they were out of view.

"I . . . don't know if I like her," Laura said.

"You know this after three minutes?" I asked.

"We form impressions within the first second of meeting someone," Laura said. "My impression is she's a lot."

"What do you mean?"

"All of that 'if you want to,' 'if you'd like to.' The gifts. I just think she wants us to like her too much."

"I like my gift," I said, flipping through my new notebook.

"Yeah, I do too," she said. "It's just—"

"I think she's kind of okay," I said. "Like, given the possible options."

"I mean, yeah, I wouldn't describe her as bad," Laura said. "There were certainly good things. She didn't talk to us like little kids, at least. She wasn't, like, grossly all over Dad."

"There was a lot of back touching," I said.

"I can deal with back touching."

"I'd like much less back and general touching."

"She didn't pinch our cheeks or hold our faces in her hands and say, 'Wow, you look just like your father.' The hug was fine. You clearly liked that."

"Shut up," I said.

"But, I don't know, there's just something about her that I don't fully like," Laura said. "And I think she's going to try to *life-coach* us."

"I didn't pick up on that."

"We can have a real *fun* time together, *if you'd like to*," Laura said in a slightly contemptuous impression of Lucrecia's voice.

It seemed like a normal statement to me, but I didn't want to get into an argument, so I just said, "Hmm, yeah."

Laura paused to think. "How would you rate her, one to ten?"

"I don't know," I said. "A six, I guess."

"That seems high," Laura said. "I'd give her a five."

# TWENTY-SEVEN

**WHEN WE ALL PILED** into the same car, Lucrecia told us that she'd planned our day as a spiritual journey that would begin with the stomach and end with the mind. According to Chinese mystics, she explained, the "qi" of the stomach controls the rest of the body's organs. Without balanced qi, your stomach cannot properly digest food, and your mind cannot properly digest feelings and emotions.

In other words, we were going to lunch. We pulled into the heart of Terlingua: Eddie's Edible Tex-Mex. As soon as we were seated, Dad excused himself to the restroom. You'd think he'd understand that he was the glue of the table, the only connection between us and the woman sitting across from us, and therefore shouldn't immediately leave the three of us alone together. But no. He hopped up without a care and left us face-to-face with Lucrecia.

At least I had the menu to block the direct connection between our faces. I picked mine up and pretended to read while waiting for Laura to say something. But she was utilizing the same technique, and we sat in awkward fake menu contemplation for at least a minute.

Then Lucrecia gently set down her menu. "I understand that you may be feeling a little . . . uncomfortable."

I put down my menu and nodded. Though I felt more than just uncomfortable. I was also feeling anxious, nervous, vaguely angry, and, in some sense, excited. Every feeling mixed together, and the combined effect was a headache and an uneasy, fluttering stomach.

"I am too," Lucrecia said. "It's nothing to feel bad about. But I do have a little exercise we could try to maybe move through some of this discomfort. How does that sound?"

We agreed, happy that she was prepared to fill the silence without mentioning stomach qi again.

"Wonderful," she said, clasping her hands together in excitement. "There's a few steps to this exercise, so you'll have to follow along. First, I'll need you to both close your eyes."

We looked at her uncertainly.

"It's okay," she said. "This isn't some trick. I'm not going to do anything. Just close your eyes."

We did.

"Now," Lucrecia continued, "I want you to experience the darkness behind your eyes. *Sit* in the darkness. Feel it, in full."

We sat in the darkness. It felt like closing your eyes in a restaurant.

"Do you feel it?" she asked gently.

I was still feeling mostly nauseous, but nodded yes.

"Now Laura, I'd like for you to think about Theo. And Theo, you think about Laura."

My immediate mental image was of Laura yelling at me and slamming her bedroom door.

"Keep thinking. As you think, I want you to pick three words that you'd use to describe each other. You don't have to think very deeply, just the first three words that come to mind."

The first three words that came to mind were "loud," "annoying," and "smart."

"Do you have your words ready?" Lucrecia asked.

I nodded.

"Now open your eyes," Lucrecia said. She gestured for Laura to go first.

"Theo is . . . creative . . . smart . . . and patient," Laura said with a mischievous smile.

"That's so sweet," Lucrecia cooed.

I immediately understood what Laura was doing and had to bite the inside of my cheek to keep from laughing. I tried to up the ante even further. "When I think of Laura," I said, "the first three words that come to mind are intelligent, thoughtful, and the last one is more of a phrase, but I hope it still counts: a gentle soul."

Laura started laughing and Lucrecia joined in. I wasn't sure if she was in on the joke or just trying to show that we were all having a good time together.

"You two are so *kind* to each other," Lucrecia said. "I was honestly expecting some more friction since your father told me you were always fighting."

"Dad said we're always fighting?" Laura asked.

"If I remember correctly, his exact words were 'almost always fighting,'" she said as Dad returned, sliding into the booth next to her. "Isn't that right? You told me they were 'almost always fighting'?"

"I don't know if I used those *exact* words," Dad said.

"I think you did," Lucrecia said. "It may have been a radically honest moment."

"What's a radically honest moment?" Laura asked.

"It's a sort of exercise where you are completely honest and say exactly what you're thinking," Lucrecia answered.

"And *Dad* does this?" Laura asked.

"He loves it," Lucrecia said, beaming in Dad's direction. He sheepishly smiled.

"Can we try it?" Laura asked with real interest.

"If everyone wants to," Lucrecia said.

Dad's face reddened and he said quietly, "I don't know if this is the right place to —"

"Radical honesty," Laura said, slapping her palm on the table. "Dad's trying to change the subject because he doesn't like to talk to us about serious things. Especially in restaurants. When we go out to eat he only talks about, like, what's hanging on the walls and how much things cost."

"Very good!" Lucrecia said, admirably pointing a finger in Laura's direction and then over to Dad, signaling his turn for a 100 percent honest response.

Dad sighed. "Radical honesty: I just want to order lunch."

"Boooo," Laura said.

"He's being honest," Lucrecia said, gently patting Dad's shoulder and ensuring him he'd done a good job. "Theo, it's your turn. Speak your truth," she prompted.

"Um, okay," I said. "My truth is that I know that Dad would like me to order the grilled cheese because it's the cheapest thing on the menu, but I would rather order whatever I want without thinking about the price."

"My truth," Dad said, setting down the menu and entering the game, "is if you order something over ten dollars, you're paying for it."

"My truth is I don't have any money," I said.

"*My* truth," Lucrecia said, "is that Theo can order whatever he wants and I'll pay for it."

"You don't have to do that," Dad said.

"I'm happy to," Lucrecia said, winking at me.

I was not expecting a wink and instinctively scowled, but did appreciate the sentiment.

"Can you pay for me, too?" Laura asked.

"Let's not push it," Dad said sharply.

"I would be happy to pay for everyone's meal," Lucrecia said. "Order whatever you'd like."

I ordered the most expensive item on the menu: a seasoned sirloin steak burrito with loaded nachos. It was, honestly, one of the best things I've ever eaten.

# TWENTY-EIGHT

**THE NEXT STOP** on Lucrecia's planned spiritual journey was the Desert Lotus Healing Arts Center, a collection of words that weren't in Dad's vocabulary. Here, she explained, we would be assisted in radiating our positive stomach qi outward to the rest of our bodies. She went on like this for a few minutes. I didn't fully understand what she was saying, but was looking forward to the radiating part. I pictured my body glowing and shooting out lasers in every direction, which seemed exciting.

As we got closer, I recognized our destination as the place with the giant dinosaur sculpture that we passed earlier. We turned and parked next to a small building covered in swirling flower patterns.

Inside, a large granite ball painted like the world rested in the center of a fountain. Its lightly splashing water competed with the sound of falling rain piped in from what I guessed was a falling rain playlist. Behind the fountain was a large desk and a mural of the sun hugging the moon. Beneath the mural sat a middle-aged woman wearing an impeccably white dress, her wrists and neck covered in band upon band of different-colored rocks and pendants.

"You must be the Lou . . . creek . . . iaa party," the woman behind the desk struggled to read while maintaining an effervescent smile.

"*Lucrecia*, yes," Lucrecia said.

"My apologies, *Lucrecia*. It's so lovely to have you here today. My name's Infinity and I'll be taking care of you at the start of your journey."

"Journey?" I whisper-asked Dad.

"We're getting massages," he whispered. "She's paying."

Infinity flicked a miniature gong on the corner of her desk, and four people in white robes appeared from behind a beaded curtain: two very thin middle-aged women with severely wrapped hair, a college-aged woman with tattoos of vegetables covering both arms, and a burly older man with long gray hair.

"Theo?" the older man called.

"That's me," I said sheepishly.

"The name's Dusk," he said, taking and crushing my hand in his. "You'll be with me."

"Um," I said.

"Go on," Lucrecia urged. "You're in good hands with Dusk."

I followed Dusk down a narrow hallway to a side room painted bright sky blue. In the center of the room was a small bed with a cutout hole to rest your head. In the corner was a chair with a robe draped across it. He closed the door and motioned for me to sit in the chair.

"I understand that this will be your first massage experience," he said in a calm and gentle voice. "There's no need to be nervous. I'll walk you through the basics. The first thing we'll need to do is settle on the musical accompaniment." He pulled an index card from his robe pocket. "There are several options to choose from: Peaceful Stream, Cloud over Mountain, Nature's Kiss, and Eagle's Flight. Which of those strikes you as best?"

None of them struck me. "Do you have any, like, rock music?" I asked.

"Um . . . I might have some Grateful Dead on my phone."

"Absolutely not," I said instinctively.

Dusk winced as if deeply hurt.

"I'm sorry," I said. "I didn't mean to insult you. My dad's a big Grateful Dead fan. It's not really my thing."

"Your dad sounds like a good man," Dusk said.

"Sure," I said. I'd already forgotten most of the musical options, so agreed to the only one I could remember: Nature's Kiss.

"Perfect," Dusk said, checking off a box on his index card. "Now, I'll need you to *change* before we get started. Don't worry, I'll step outside for a minute. You can undress to whatever level you're comfortable with and then go ahead and lie down on the bed. Do you have any questions for me before I step out?"

I had a lot of questions, but said, "No, sounds good."

He stepped out of the room and turned on a series of low-volume bird calls and wind noises that must have been Nature's Kiss. The sounds, combined with the song's title, briefly caused me to picture Leonard's face puckering into a kiss. I then used every ounce of mental strength to push that image out of my mind.

I looked over at the robe hanging on the chair and considered my disrobing options. I wasn't comfortable taking off any of my clothes to any level, but figured I had to at least take off my shirt or he'd think I was weird. So I took off my shirt and stood in my underwear, shorts, and socks.

I decided my socks could also go and remained in underwear and shorts. That's about the same level of clothing for swimming, and I've been swimming hundreds of times without feeling uncomfortable, but swimming seems different from lying down on a bed while an old man rubbed my shoulders.

I lay down on the bed and struggled to fit my face in the cutout face hole, as there wasn't a convenient place to put my nose. While I continuously readjusted my face, a knock and "Theo?" rang from the door.

"Yes," I said through the uncomfortable hole.

Dusk opened the door and walked in. I was staring at the floor and wasn't sure if I was supposed to raise my head back up to acknowledge Dusk or continue staring at the floor. I decided to continue staring at the floor.

"Your mother said that your family is very *tense*," he said.

"She's not my mother," I said to the floor.

"I'm sorry?"

"She's not my mother," I said more loudly.

"My mistake. Your . . . friend said you've had a long week of hiking and needed to relax a little. To release all that tension and welcome the gentle flow of the universe back into your tendons."

I didn't know what to say, so I just said, "Yeah."

He put his hands on my back and I flinched. My shoulders shot up to my ears like a turtle protecting its neck.

"Reeelllaaxxxx," he said in a singsongy voice. He tried to push my shoulders down but my body fought against him. "You have to *relax*," he said again.

I tried, but it's hard to relax when you're being told to relax.

"Let your body go loose," he said.

I remained hunched.

"Try breathing," Dusk suggested. He leaned in close to my ear and took a deep breath. "Like this. Innnn. Ouutttttt."

I tried to breathe in deeply and started coughing uncontrollably.

"Let it out, let it out," he said, taking my shoulders and pushing them out of their natural hunch. "There we go."

The coughing fit had lowered my guard and Dusk was now in control. He began circling the area where my backpack had hung on my shoulders. Did it still feel kind of weird? Yes. Did it also feel like taking the best, most perfectly warm and relaxing shower without the water ever cooling or your body ever pruning? Yes. After ten minutes, I understood why rich people were always at spas. After half an hour, I resolved to become rich and live at a spa.

At the end of the hour, my new best friend Dusk gave me a complimentary bathing suit and led me outdoors to a soaking pool where Laura, Dad, and Lucrecia were already lounging. Their peaceful, natural smiles reflected my own current feelings. I slipped into the water and let the circulating bubbles wash over me. We were all in a state of such complete satisfaction that no one had the mental energy to construct sentences. Instead, we spent five minutes trading adjectives about how we felt.

"Terrific," Dad said.

"Wonderful," Laura said.

"Amazing," Lucrecia said.

"Incredible," I said.

"Fantastic," Dad said.

"Stupendous," Laura said.

"Marvelous," Lucrecia said.

I couldn't think of any other words, so we sat in peaceful quiet for several minutes.

"I want to keep sitting here for hours," Laura said.

"Your body is radiating pure positive qi," Lucrecia said. "Your muscles and tendons are shaking hands beneath your skin."

Picturing my muscles and tendons shaking hands beneath my skin somewhat killed the mood, but I closed my eyes and focused on the sensation of the warm bubbles traveling against my legs.

"I could get used to this," Dad said.

"We could start booking monthly massages," Lucrecia said.

"Who is we?" Laura said.

"All of us, together," Lucrecia said.

"I could certainly get used to that," Dad said.

# TWENTY-NINE

**AFTER SOAKING** for another hour, we changed and reboarded the car. Having addressed the needs of our bodies, Lucrecia said, it was time to nourish the mind. Terlingua Ghost Town didn't have a library but did have a museum, so we continued our tour of non-Dad destinations at the Museum of Contemporary Art.

It had been a while since I'd been to an art museum. Mom used to take us to the museum in downtown Austin once a year. It was free on Sundays and there was always something new to see. As far as I can remember, Dad joined us only once and spent the entire time making fun of everything and coming up with fake titles for all the paintings. I think he touched a sculpture too. More than one sculpture and a few precious artifacts. He was never invited again and museum visits became strictly Laura, Mom, and me events.

"Contemporary art can be *challenging*," Lucrecia told us on the way in, "but you must not be intimidated. If you allow yourself to *engage* with the art, I promise that it will be rewarding."

In the lobby was a painting of a cowboy decomposing in a barren desert.

"Such a striking image," Lucrecia said.

I waited for Dad to make a joke but instead he said "Very

powerful." He and Lucrecia joined hands and continued to the front desk.

"Very powerful?" I whispered to Laura.

"It *is* a powerful statement about the necessary death of the cowboy myth," she said. "Don't be a philistine."

Because we were the only people at the museum, the front desk offered a free guided tour. A petite elderly woman with expensive-looking earrings and a dark blue pantsuit led us into the first room.

"This is our local art section," she said in a voice that sounded like someone from Texas using a British accent. "We're very fortunate to have some exceptional artists in West Texas."

The room was mostly empty. On one wall was a row of neon light bulbs stacked from floor to ceiling. In the center of the room was a series of painted plastic boxes, one for each color of the rainbow. I tried to engage with the art but didn't feel particularly challenged or nourished by neon lights and plastic boxes. Once again, I waited for Dad to make a joke, but instead he slowly walked around, nodded respectfully, and, using his own nearly British voice, said, "A remarkable usage of . . . lights and, uh, color."

"And such beautiful use of the room's blank space," Lucrecia added, squeezing his hand.

"Truly marvelous," Dad agreed.

Laura and I rolled our eyes at each other, which the tour guide unfortunately saw.

"Often *underappreciated* by *children*," she said, ineffectively trying to shame us, "this room showcases a real *passion* for creation. The lights that you see were carefully handcrafted by the artist over six years."

"Very impressive," Dad said.

"Such dedication," Lucrecia said.

*I want to leave,* I said in my head.

"If you'll follow me," the tour guide said, "our second room houses a visiting exhibition called the Limits of Seeing."

We trailed behind her into the next room, which looked like it was under construction. In the middle of the room was a series of industrial ladders connecting metal platforms that gradually led up to a skylight in the ceiling.

I walked around the room cautiously, wondering what it was supposed to mean. Then the guide said it was an interactive exhibit that I could climb up if I wanted. Laura and I immediately raced to the bottom ladder and began our ascent as the loving couple remained below, listening to the guide drone on about the uniqueness of the something whatever something.

We climbed through the maze of ladders and platforms to the top, where a telescope pointed up at the skylight. I looked into it and saw nothing—total blackness.

"I can't see anything," I told Laura.

"I think the top's covered," she said, craning her neck to inspect the end of the telescope.

"Can you take it off?" I asked.

She struggled to twist and pry the cap off. "I think it's

permanently covered." She tried with all her might to pop the cap off again. "It's glued shut or something."

"We climbed all the way up here to look at nothing?"

"The Limits of Seeing," she said.

"What?" I said.

"That's the title of this thing. Remember?"

I deeply exhaled. "This kind of art sucks," I said, spinning the telescope knob to no effect. "Give me a painting of some-one's face any day over this."

"I'll give you a painting of your face," Laura said.

"Good one."

"Thank you."

"I guess we should go back down?" I said.

"No, wait," Laura said, putting her hand in front of my chest to stop me from descending the stupid covered-telescope platform. "Look."

Our current position was the perfect place to watch Dad and Lucrecia without them seeing us. The guide had left the room and they were whispering back and forth.

"I love art so much. It's just so *artistic,* don't you think," Laura said, imitating Dad.

"I'm radiating pure positive qi by looking at this ladder," I said, imitating Lucrecia.

"My qi is really—" Laura started, but abruptly stopped because Dad and Lucrecia weren't talking anymore. They were kissing.

It wasn't a kiss like the little pecks he used to give Mom. This was a movie kiss. A swirling camera kiss. A disgusting kiss.

I stopped breathing. I looked over at Laura to see how she was doing breathing-wise. She was also struggling. We exchanged glances of horror.

I don't know how to fully express how I felt. To watch him all dressed up, pretending to like art he didn't understand, and then slipping his tongue into a woman's mouth? It was too much for one day.

"I think I'm going to throw up," Laura said.

I guess that expressed my feelings pretty well.

# THIRTY

**I HAVE TROUBLE PRETENDING** things are fine when they're not. During the car ride back, I didn't say anything but the occasional "yeah" to act like I was involved in whatever conversation was going on. I heard enough to understand that Dad and Lucrecia were going out to a local theater that night while Laura and I would be left alone to order dinner from the one restaurant that delivered.

When we got back, I pretended to take a nap while Dad changed into his third outfit of the day, a new record. I knew he could sense something was up, but I didn't want to talk about it, so I turned and faced the wall before he came back into the room. That way he couldn't as easily see that I was fake-napping. And that I had one earbud in because fake-napping gets boring after five minutes.

I could tell by his hesitant footsteps in my direction that he was considering gently shaking me awake, so I remained still and concentrated on breathing up and down in a sleeping-like fashion. He slowly retreated and climbed the ladder up to Laura's loft.

I listened as he explained to Laura that he wasn't going on a date. That it was just a chance for him and Lucrecia to spend some time alone, and it would also give us a chance to spend some time alone. That we could do whatever we wanted as long as we didn't go more than one hundred feet away from the house. That there were coyotes in the area that tended to come out at night and we should probably stay inside once it got dark.

Laura responded yeah, whatever, who cares.

Dad explained that Laura was the one in charge. That this was a serious responsibility and she should be listening, not just saying yeah, whatever.

She explained duh, yeah, she was listening, get off her back, didn't he have to leave soon?

After Dad shut the front door, I grabbed my phone and texted Angel P.

**ME:** My dad has a girlfriend
And she's here
👻

**ANGEL P.:** are u serious?
like a real girlfriend?

**ME:** She seems very real

**ANGEL P.:** real good looking?

**ME:** She's fine, whatever

**ANGEL P.:** i bet shes fine

**ME:** She's a normal looking person

**ANGEL P.:** ugly then?

**ME:** No, she's not ugly. That's not really the point.

**ANGEL P.:** the point is ur dads a player

**ME:** Ew, no

**ANGEL P.:** 😎

u got battle crash yet?

**ME:** No, obviously

**ANGEL P.:** get on it bruh

I don't know why I expected more from Angel P. Most of our conversations were about other people at school or the games he played well. And I know that during the summer, he's online fourteen hours a day and rarely texts back.

I didn't respond and instead started searching for "dad dating new girlfriend." There were two streams to follow: posts from people in my situation and posts from dads giving advice to one another on websites like divorceddads.com, thebroken-family.org, and widowdad.net. Exactly the kind of top-search-result websites that Dad would read. Hoping to glean some of the advice he had no doubt read and absorbed, I clicked on an article titled "Seven Steps to Successfully Prepare Your Children for Meeting Your New Girlfriend" from divorceddads.com.

He'd followed most of the steps. He'd waited over six months before letting us know that he was dating. (Which seemed like bad advice, probably not the kind of advice that marrieddads.com would give.) He had tried to create a "fun climate" for the first meeting. (What's more fun than the fifth day of a family vacation in the Texas desert?) He hadn't "forced" us into liking her. (He had somewhat forced us.)

What he hadn't followed was the last step, the thing that was bothering me the most: be yourself. In his one day of visibly dating, he had become an entirely different person, and not one I particularly liked.

I heard Laura shifting upstairs and decided to go back to fake sleep. She climbed down the ladder and stood at the foot of my bed. "I know you're fake-sleeping," she said.

I didn't move.

"Cool," she said.

She went into the kitchen and ordered a pizza. My fake-sleeping must have slipped into the real thing because I was startled awake by the loud knock of the pizza delivery man.

"You're welcome," Laura said as I stumbled into the kitchen. She was looking through the cupboards for plates, but there weren't any. She shrugged and set the box down on the center of the table. We each took a giant slice of pizza, using our hands as plates.

I was restored from my surprise nap and ready to dissect our first eight hours with Lucrecia.

"So," I said, "that kiss."

"I don't want to talk about it," she said.

"We have to talk about it," I said.

"No, we don't. We're eating."

"That wasn't a 'we're just talking' kiss or a 'this is just a test' kiss," I said, ignoring her. "That was a 'this is a serious relation-ship' kiss."

"You know different kiss classifications?" she said.

"You know what I'm saying," I said.

"No, I don't," she said.

"Yes, you do," I said. "You're the one with kiss experience."

"Shut up," she said.

"Make me," I said.

She threw her pizza crust at my face.

"Was it José?" I asked, unfazed by the crust ricocheting off my forehead. He and Laura used to be friends before he mysteriously stopped coming by our house a year ago.

"Ew, no. I'm not telling!" Laura said.

"Fine," I said. "I'm just saying that Dad lied to us. He and Lucrecia are *involved*."

Laura picked up another slice of pizza. "I don't know why you're surprised."

"There was also that stuff at the spa," I said. "'We could do this once a month.' 'I could get used to this.'"

"I could get used to that part," Laura said. "The going-to-spas part is fine with me."

"I could too, obviously," I said. "But what are we supposed to do about the rest?"

"What do you mean *do?* There's nothing to do. Dad's going to do whatever he wants," she said. She took a bite of her pizza. "I mean, I don't think she's *that* bad."

"She's okay, but do you really want to be with her and Dad *every day?* This was just one day. Imagine this always."

"Even if it's serious, it's not like she's going to move in next week."

"But she could move in *in a year*."

"That still seems too fast for Dad," she said. "And by then

who cares. I'd only have one more year and then I'll be gone anyways."

"But I can't leave," I said. "I'd have to live with them for *four years.*"

"Sucks for you." She tossed another pizza crust at my forehead.

I threw it back at her. "Just because you'll be in college doesn't mean she won't be your mom too."

"*Step*mom," she said.

"You're fine with having a new *step*mom?" I said, my voice rising with each word.

"Calm down," she said. "It's only been one day."

"Why are you being all 'I don't care' about this?" I said.

"Because it *doesn't matter,*" she said angrily. "Dad will give some speech about how our feelings are important and this is a family decision that we all have to blah blah blah, but he'll do what he wants."

"He's not always like that," I said.

"*Yes,* he is. He is *always like that.*"

"Maybe if you weren't arguing with him all the time, he'd listen to you more."

"Don't turn this around on me," she said. "You wanted my opinion. I gave it to you."

"I don't like your opinion," I said.

"I don't care."

Laura left the kitchen and stomped upstairs to text for four hours.

I went out on the porch and tried to work on *Bob: The Boy with Perfect Memory.* I flipped to where I'd left off. Bob was recounting the happiest days of his life as they were projected on a screen. I looked at my drawings of Bob and his mom celebrating a birthday party and laughing together at the movies and it all felt stupid. I ripped out the last two pages and threw them onto the ground. Then I tossed my notebook down, took a deep breath, and looked out at the dark, empty desert.

Before Mom died, Laura and I used to talk to each other all the time. She'd come into my bedroom at night and sit at the foot of my bed and start talking. She'd tell me about all the drama with her friends or which teachers she hated. Sometimes she would try to give me advice, which I outwardly ignored but secretly followed. During the year Mom was sick, we'd compare the different things she said to us, and try to use them as a gauge for how well Mom was feeling. After these conversations, I always felt more comfortable and less worried about the future. But it had been over a year since Laura had visited my room. Our conversations rarely lasted longer than five minutes these days.

I was hoping that we were going to have one of those talks again. Where I could express what had been running through my mind for the past few hours. I wanted to say that if Dad married someone now, she could be our stepmom for fifty years. That those fifty years could completely erase the memories of Mom that were already starting to slip away. That while I could still remember the feelings, most of the actual experiences with

Mom had become hazy. That I couldn't recall specifics unless they were connected to a picture, but I took all the old pictures off my phone because looking at them only made me cry.

That I wasn't ready to let go of Mom's memory just yet, and her pretending like it wasn't a big deal was a lie.

# THIRTY-ONE

**ALL NIGHT LONG,** the sound of heavy rain and yelping coyotes sailed in through the window. I don't know when Dad got back, but when a particularly terrifying coyote call pierced through my light sleep, he was lying in the bed next to mine. I wanted to ask him when he'd gotten back, but he was already asleep and contentedly snoring. I also had to go to the bathroom for most of the night, but feared the coyotes would get me if I stepped foot outside. I closed my eyes and eventually somewhat slept.

In the morning it was still pouring. From the window it looked like a never-ending car wash. I suggested we take the weather as a sign that we'd overstayed our welcome, that today was the day we were, in fact, meant to leave.

"We have, in fact, paid for tonight," Dad said. "So we are, in fact, staying here until tomorrow morning."

"I am, in fact, going back to sleep," Laura said.

"You can't go back to sleep," Dad said. "Lucrecia's going to be here any minute and she said she has a surprise for us."

"I'm sick of surprises," Laura said.

"I'm sick of everything," I said.

"What's gotten into you two?" Dad asked.

Before either of us could answer, Lucrecia stumbled through the front door. She was covered head-to-toe in a camouflage poncho like a puke-colored ghost. She briskly whipped off her poncho and stood before us with an armload of board games.

"There's a whole closet full of them next door," she said. "We can play all day if we have to."

"What a *wonderful* idea!" Dad said in that tone that meant we were supposed to agree and thank her.

"It's an idea," Laura said.

"Uh-huh," I said.

We started with the Game of Life. It's one of those games like Monopoly where it's kind of fun but also you have to pay property taxes. In the board-game version of my life, I became a dentist, married, had two children, but made some bad investments along the way and eventually retired with nothing.

Laura ended up unmarried, a zoologist who became an unexpected celebrity and was able to retire to a Millionaire's Mansion.

Dad and Lucrecia ended up constantly making eyes at each other, holding hands under the table, and laughing at everything the other said.

Laura and I were still mad at each other, or at least I was still mad at her and she seemed mad at everyone, including me. But being forced to witness the spectacle of Dad and Lucrecia openly flirting had momentarily ended our feud. We set aside our differences and telepathically communicated that this was one of the worst things we'd ever had to endure.

I was nearing a breaking point and tried to calm myself by slowly counting down the remaining hours of the day I was expected to be awake. By the end of the Game of Life, there were only eleven hours left until I could reasonably go to bed. And then it would be Sunday and we'd be on our way home.

From Life, we moved on to a contentious game of Scrabble, which I also lost (third place). My highest word score was "quit," but we didn't. With the rain starting to slow and expected to stop soon, we agreed to play one last game: something called Loaded Questions that Lucrecia said was one of her favorites.

The setup was simple. There was a four-sided die with a different color on each side and four stacks of corresponding cards, one for each color. Whatever color you rolled, you had to take the top card from that pile and read the question aloud. Everyone else writes their answer down on a slip of paper. Then the answers are shuffled and read aloud. The person who rolled guesses who wrote what. For every correct guess, they get to move one space forward. The first person to make it to the end of the board wins.

"Let's do a practice round," Lucrecia said, happily sliding slips of paper to each of us. "I'll read the question and you all write your answers down."

She picked the first card from the orange pile and read, "'What do you wish you could stop from happening?'"

"The answers are anonymous, right?" Laura asked.

"Yes," Lucrecia said. "Don't put your name on the paper. Just write your answer."

I wrote, *I wish I could stop Laura from existing,* and slid my paper face-down toward Lucrecia.

After Dad and Laura slid their own answers her way, Lucrecia carefully shuffled them. "Here we go," she said. "The question was 'What do you wish you could stop from happening?'" She picked up the first slip of paper and said, "We have 'I wish I could stop this vacation from ending.' Aw, that's sweet. I think I know who wrote this one." She smiled sickeningly in Dad's direction before picking up the next slip. "And this one says, 'I wish I could stop Laura from existing.'"

"Hey!" Laura said.

"I'm just reading what it says," Lucrecia said. "I have a pretty good idea who wrote that one, too. And the last one says, 'I wish I could stop Dad from wearing his stupid, fake clothes.'"

Laura and I both started laughing. Even Lucrecia smiled a little bit. Dad's face turned red and he made a "tsk" sound with his tongue while trying to prevent himself from showing any flashes of real anger in front of Lucrecia.

Lucrecia reassuringly patted his knee and said, "This is fun, right?"

"Uh-huh," Dad mumbled through a pained half smile.

"I like it so far," Laura said.

"I'm a fan," I said.

"But you're making it a little too easy," Lucrecia said. "During the real game, try not to make it so obvious who's writing what."

"And let's remember to keep up our best behavior," Dad added.

Laura and I exchanged eye rolls across the table.

Dad caught it and tried to communicate *knock it off* with his eyes while his mouth struggled to maintain a smile.

As the youngest person at the table, I got to go first. I rolled purple, picked the first card from the purple pile, and read: "'What is one thing you were terribly wrong about?'"

"Let's keep these appropriate," Dad preemptively warned the table while glaring at Laura.

I looked over at Laura and saw a gleam in her eye that meant she was about to do the exact opposite. She quickly scribbled something on her slip of paper and passed it over to me. I kept it face-down until Dad and Lucrecia added theirs, and then shuffled them all together.

"The question was 'What is one thing you were terribly wrong about?'" I said. "The first one says, 'That love only comes once.'"

"Eww," Laura said with revulsion.

Dad winked at Lucrecia.

I dropped the paper like it was a piece of trash and picked up the next answer. "This one says, 'That I can handle jalapeño peppers.'"

Dad laughed heartily, apparently sharing some inside joke with Lucrecia, who was also busting up at her attempt at humor.

I picked up the last slip of paper. "And this one says, 'I was terribly wrong about Dad's intelligence. Turns out he's a great big idiot.'" I struggled to read the last four words over an uncontrollable burst of laughter. I looked over at Laura, who was doubled over in her own hysterical laughing fit.

Dad's face turned the color of lava and he looked at Laura with a mix of anger, embarrassment, or both. It was honestly hard to read the features on his boiling face. Laura stopped laughing and the room tensed as we all waited for Dad's reaction. A vein in his neck was throbbing and it looked like his jaw was ticking. He opened his mouth to speak but Lucrecia cut in instead.

"It's all right," Lucrecia said warmly, gently rubbing Dad's back as the color of his face returned to slightly sunburned. "They're just kidding. You don't really think your father is an idiot, right?" she asked Laura.

"I'm just playing the game," Laura said matter-of-factly while trying to suppress a smile.

"See?" Lucrecia said. "It's all in fun. Let's go the next round. Theo, I think you can probably guess who wrote what?"

"Um," I said. "You wrote the jalapeño thing, Dad wrote the thing about love, and Laura wrote about how Dad's a big idiot?"

Dad deeply inhaled and exhaled while gripping his left knee.

"That's right!" Lucrecia said. "Move forward three spaces."

I moved my piece forward three spaces and then passed the die over to Dad.

"Could we maybe move on to another game?" he asked.

"Come on," Lucrecia said. "Let's just do one more round. It's your roll."

Dad smiled at her weakly, rolled, and picked up the top card from the blue pile. "'What's a silly thing to brag about?'" he read.

"That's a good one!" Lucrecia said, quickly jotting something down and carefully sliding her paper in Dad's direction. They joined hands at the corner of the table and began lightly rubbing their thumbs against each other. It made me physically ill.

I looked down at my paper and wrote, *It's silly to brag about your secret girlfriend*. I shoved it across the table and Dad started to shuffle.

The disgusting hand rubbing had briefly revived his mood. With a growing smile, he picked up the first answer slip. "The question was 'What's a silly thing to brag about?' And we have 'It's silly to brag about a free vacation that isn't actually free.'"

His smile dropped and in a low voice he said, "Thank you, Laura."

"You're welcome," she said brightly.

He picked up the next answer, looked at it, and paused.

I knew that he was holding my paper and tried to remain calm as I waited for his reaction.

He continued looking down at the slip of paper in his hand. "Did you write this, Theo?" he asked through gritted teeth.

"I don't know," I said cautiously. "You'd have to read it."

He looked at me with bruising intensity and said, "I'm not going to read it."

"What does it say?" Laura asked eagerly.

"Why don't we go talk in the other room," Dad said with the same overly calm menace.

I realized that I had pushed it too far. He could take insults from Laura, but not from both of us at the same time.

"Hey, what's going on here?" Lucrecia said to Dad in a warm voice. "I'm sure it's not that bad." She plucked the paper out of his hand. Her perma-smile briefly dipped but never fully fell from her face.

"He's just kidding," she said quietly.

"He's *not* kidding!" Dad said.

"Yes, I am," I said untruthfully. "Calm down."

"Don't tell me to calm down!" he said.

*"What does it say?"* Laura asked again.

"It's none of your business," Dad said.

"It's part of the game," Laura said.

"Stay out of it," Dad said.

"What did *I* do?" Laura said.

"Look!" I interrupted, pointing toward the window.

"What?" Dad snarled.

"It stopped . . . raining," I said meekly.

They all looked toward the kitchen window. A patch of light shone on the counter, and the hazy outline of a rainbow spread through the sky.

"Perfect timing," Lucrecia said cheerily. "Now we can all lighten up a little." She squeezed Dad's hand and looked at him imploringly.

Dad eyed me with disgust and said, "Game over."

# THIRTY-TWO

**DAD HAD ALREADY DECIDED** on our afternoon plan and made us stick to it. We piled into the car and headed back to Big Bend for the last time.

It wasn't the most pleasant car ride. He gripped the steering wheel and stared straight ahead without speaking. Laura lay down in the back seat and listened to music with headphones. Lucrecia lightly hummed to show that she was still in bright spirits. That left me to once again look out the window and appreciate our final journey through the park. Slicked with rain and haloed by a rainbow, the buttes and sand dunes did have a certain beauty. But not enough to lift me out of my foul mood.

We were making our way toward Santa Elena Canyon, the "Lovers' Lane" of the park, where you could raft or kayak down a stretch of the Rio Grande that passed between two mountains. As we got nearer, I recognized the surroundings as another famous photo spot. It was where fossils had been discovered, and it looked like the kind of place where dinosaurs could still live. The grass was ten feet tall, the rocks were massive, and the two mountains jutted monstrously into the sky. It was so immediately impressive that as we pulled into the dirt parking lot, Dad broke his silence and uttered a single word: "Wow."

And then Lucrecia said, "Wow is right, darling," and squeezed his hand.

With only four words and one hand gesture, my mood swung from momentary amazement back to deep annoyance.

Not that it mattered. We continued to follow Dad's plan without discussion. He marched us forward to the raft rental station, a makeshift tent next to a rickety table where a woman sat in casual military-style gear and wraparound sunglasses.

"New recruits?!" she barked, but also it was a question.

"Four recruits ready for service," Dad said, accompanied by an embarrassing salute. He was trying to cover his anger by being overly cheerful and was giving off a kind of wild, unhinged vibe.

"Y'all got any water-crafting slash water-sporting experience?" the woman asked, still sitting and judging us from behind her sunglasses.

I had been canoeing once as a Cub Scout, but only lasted twenty minutes before tipping over into the water. Since then, I hadn't attempted any water-crafting slash water-sporting experiences.

"We're *largely* inexperienced, but we do have one member in our party," Dad said, indicating Lucrecia, "who's braved the rapids of the Mississippi River."

"The Mississippi doesn't have rapids," the woman corrected.

"Who's braved the *swiftly rushing waters* of the Mississippi," Dad said.

The woman shook her head. "Y'all are greenhorns. Nothing wrong with that."

"Excuse me?" Dad said.

"Greenhorns. People inexperienced and untrained to undertake a certain endeavor. In this case, maneuvering a raft down the Rio Grande."

"I guess you're right, then. Four *greenhorns* ready for service," Dad said, saluting again.

She remained blank-faced for several seconds before shouting to no one in particular, "Two kayaks!"

Two men leaped out from behind the grass, each carrying a long kayak and two paddles.

"This will have to do for today," the woman said. "I assume you don't mind splitting up?"

"No, that would be great!" Dad said.

He turned toward Laura and me. He told us that this would be the perfect opportunity for each of us to spend some "quality alone time" with Lucrecia. On the way out, she and I would share a kayak. On the way back, she and Laura would share a kayak. Though he delivered this with a smile, he made it very clear with his eyes that he'd refuse to answer any questions or listen to any dissenting opinions. We *would* kayak down Lovers' Lane with his girlfriend, like it or not.

At least in a kayak you don't sit face-to-face. I was in the back spot facing Lucrecia's hair, which you'd think would slightly deter her from continually turning her head to talk over her shoulder. But no. She was very comfortable turning her head around like an owl, looking forward to monitor our course with one eye while looking directly at me with the other.

"Your father," Lucrecia said. "Do you mind if I call him 'your father'? Would you prefer something like 'your dad' or 'Stanley'?"

"Whatever," I said.

"I'll stick with 'your father,' then," she said. "*Your father* said you were named after the inventor of the laser?"

"Yeah, that's a joke he tells," I said.

"It isn't true?"

"I don't know."

"Well, it's quite interesting — names. Don't you think?"

"I guess so."

"My name, for example, comes from my father's family in Argentina. It's considered a quite beautiful name there. Though I've spent most of my life correcting people here." She lightly laughed at her semi-joke.

"Cool," I said.

We silently paddled for the next minute or two, her head still turned with one ear angled in my direction expectantly, waiting for me to take up some of the conversational slack. I didn't, and the time continued to pass glacially. I was trying to count down from forty-five minutes in my head, but every minute felt like five and her turned ear was making me anxious.

"The mountains are . . . nice," I eventually said.

"Spectacular!" she eagerly responded. "And the water is so clear."

"Yeah," I said.

That covered the nature talk. We sat in silence for another minute.

"Have you enjoyed your time in Big Bend?" she asked.

"It's been pretty good," I said.

"I'm glad to hear it," she said. "Your father was a little concerned about your enthusiasm for the trip before you left."

"Why?"

"He'd read an article about nature deficit disorder and was a little worried that maybe you had it."

"I don't have any disorders," I said.

"It's not an official disorder," she said. "It's just a new term to describe people who don't find joy in nature."

"I find joy in nature," I said.

"Well, that's excellent," she said. "That means you don't suffer from the disorder."

"I thought it wasn't a disorder."

"You're right," she said. "I mean the new term doesn't describe you."

"Dad said I didn't like nature?"

"He had some concerns."

"I like nature just fine."

"Certainly," she said. "I don't mean to question your love of nature."

More silence followed. The sound of the paddles moving through the water.

"I can understand why this is uncomfortable for you, you

know," she said after two minutes. "I'm not so old. I remember what it was like to be a teenager."

"I don't think you're old," I said.

"That's nice, but that's not really what I'm getting at," she said. "Could we maybe talk more candidly?"

"Candidly?"

"Purposefully and directly. I feel like there's a pretty sizable . . . division between us. And I can understand why you wouldn't want to close that gap. You clearly have some complicated emotions about me."

*Some complicated emotions* was a light way of saying it. "Yeah, I guess so," I said.

"And I'm willing to talk about some of those emotions with you."

"I don't really want to," I said.

She paused for a few seconds but didn't give up. "You know, I've noticed that you and your sister are very reactive, but don't really explore your emotions more deeply."

"So," I said.

"*So*, I think that's interesting," she said. "I think your father is the same way, but he's made it a goal to become more open, and I have been able to help him with that. I think he would also like to speak with *you* more openly if you'd show him that you are willing to be open too."

"I don't think that's true," I said.

"Do you see what you just did?" she said. "Your first reaction was to shut me down instead of engaging with the conversation."

"You're just trying to trick me into talking about what you want to talk about," I said.

"I'm not trying to trick you," she said in a gentle voice. "I'm trying to connect with you. To understand you. But there's a block between us."

"Okay," I said.

"And I would like to discuss that block if you're interested in having that conversation with me," she said. "Can we have that conversation?"

I didn't particularly want to but felt somewhat trapped. She had clearly made it her goal to connect with me on our forty-five-minute kayak trip and wouldn't stop until we had "connected" to her satisfaction. Because I'm not, by nature, a rude person, having to say "no" ten times in less than an hour was wearing me down.

"I mean . . . I guess so," I said.

"Now we're getting somewhere," she said, readjusting her posture. "Can I ask you some questions?"

"I said *yes,*" I said.

"Don't get defensive," she said.

"I'm not being defensive," I said.

"Good," she said, turning and smiling. "Just be honest. I want your honest responses to these questions. Okay?"

"Uh-huh," I said.

"How would you describe your emotional state right now?" she asked.

"I don't know. Good," I said.

"Good isn't an emotion."

"Is happy an emotion?" I asked.

"Of course," she said.

"Then I feel happy," I said.

"You don't *seem* happy," she said.

"I'm fine," I said.

"Fine isn't an emotion," she said.

"Can we move on?" I said.

"This isn't going to work if you don't allow yourself to be honest," she said.

"I'm *being* honest."

"Let me be more direct in my intention here," she said. "I believe that you have a lot of anger directed toward me. And I think it's likely connected to feelings about your mother that you haven't fully worked through."

I didn't know what to say, so didn't say anything.

"Your father told me about your story," she said.

"What story?"

"Bob: The Boy with the Best Memory," she said.

"The Boy with *Perfect* Memory," I corrected. I didn't know that Dad read it. I'd shown him my first graphic novel, *The Aliens Who Ate People and Never Got Full,* and his only response was "very creative," so I kept my work private from then on. He must have peeked through my notebook at some point during the past few days.

"There's real pain in that story," she said.

"It's just a story," I said.

"There's a reason Bob's worst memory is the day his mother died," she said.

I didn't say anything.

"You know, my mother died when I was eighteen," she said. "I still think about her."

"I was eleven," I said.

"I understand that it's much different."

"I don't really want to talk about it," I said.

"Talking about it is the first step toward working through those emotions."

"I *don't* want to talk about it."

"It's very difficult to talk about. I understand that. But it *will* help you to have those emotions out in the open. I *promise* that it will help."

"It's *not* helping."

She sighed, turned around to face forward, then turned back to look at me. "I just think you have all of these bottled-up feelings and you would feel so much better if you let them out."

"Can we please just paddle?" I said.

She turned around and we paddled down the rest of Lovers' Lane in silence.

# THIRTY-THREE

**LAURA AND DAD** were waiting for us on the gravelly sand at the end of the riverway. As we got closer, Dad helped pull the front of our kayak to the shore and lent a hand to lift Lucrecia out. I waved off his help and crawled out by myself. Lucrecia led him a few paces ahead to speak in hushed tones while I sidled next to Laura to commiserate.

"She tried to talk to me about Mom after ten minutes," I said.

"I knew it!" Laura said. "I *told you* she was going to use her life-coaching on us."

"You were right," I said dejectedly.

"What did you say?" she asked.

"That I didn't want to talk about it."

"She better not try that with me," Laura said.

"You know she's going to," I said. "How was Dad?"

"Terrible," she said. "He spent the first half lecturing me about how *rude* I was during Loaded Questions. Then he kept talking about the beauty of the Rio Grande and how blue the water is. Then he kept . . ."

Laura continued rattling off her complaints, but I wasn't listening. I was looking ahead at Dad and Lucrecia. He was giving her a hug, trying to comfort her, as if *she* were the one who was hurt. Like I was the person who'd dragged her into the middle of a river and started pressing her about her dead mother.

". . . but we only have six more hours, right?" Laura said, pulling me back to the conversation she was trying to have with me.

"What?" I said.

"We just need to make it through the next six hours and then the vacation's over."

"That's too long," I said.

Lucrecia and Dad turned and slowly paced toward us. His face still held a pained, aggressive smile. He told us it was time to switch partners and paddle back, but more leisurely, to best enjoy our last hour in the park.

I was again in the back of the kayak, facing Dad's burned neck. Unlike Lucrecia, he looked straight ahead but spoke loudly, his words looping back to me on the wind. He started, as Laura had warned, by describing the blueness of the water. He then moved on to describing the beauty of the mountains. Without anything else to describe as beautiful, he hedged toward what he really wanted to talk about.

"Lucrecia told me to tell you that she's sorry. She didn't mean to offend you," he said, waiting for me to accept the apology.

I didn't say anything, so he continued, "She said she was just trying to resolve a tension."

"It's fine," I said.

"She said it didn't seem fine. It seemed like you were pretty upset."

"Well, yeah, I didn't want to talk to her about Mom, so what."

"She was just trying to help."

"I don't *want* her help."

"You could have been a little bit nicer about it."

I was tired of adults telling me what I needed to do in order to feel better and be more comfortable. They were the ones who were making me feel bad and uncomfortable. I'd never yelled at my dad before, like really *yelled* yelled, but I'd reached my limit.

"Why do *I* have to be nice to her? She's not *my* life coach. I didn't ask for her help. And why should *she* be the one to *resolve my tension* about Mom? *You're* the one who never wants to talk about anything. We've talked about it maybe three times in the past two years!"

He started to turn around to say something.

"I'm not finished!" I shouted. He closed his mouth and kept his body half-turned in my direction. Everything I'd been thinking over the past two days came tumbling out at once.

"You never even asked me if I was okay with you dating. Not that I would know what to say. I didn't have any real time to think about whether I was okay with it or not because the next day, she was here. *There*," I said, pointing thirty feet ahead of us. "And do you know what she's probably saying right now? The only thing that she can think to talk about? That Laura needs to *resolve her emotions* about Mom because she's ready to move in and take over." I paused to catch my breath. My heart was pounding in my chest, spiking in the way it does when you're speaking freely without thinking about the repercussions.

"You expect me to go along with whatever you want to do because I'm the *easy* one. I don't complain like Laura, but that doesn't mean I don't get annoyed. So no, I'm not going to accept her help and I don't want your help either. I just want to be left alone to think about what I want. When I want help, I'll ask for it."

He thought for a few moments, sharply exhaled, and stoically replied, "Thank you for sharing."

# THIRTY-FOUR

**IT FEELS GOOD** to speak the truth, but the truth often makes other people angry. Dad didn't say another word to me for the rest of our time at the park. I couldn't tell whether he was angry, hurt, or sad, because he wasn't communicating anything.

When we got back to the houses in Terlingua, he and Lucrecia huddled outside for a few minutes as Laura and I went inside. When he opened the front door and joined us in the kitchen, he announced that our planned all-you-can-eat-buffet dinner was canceled. He delivered the news like someone at a press conference reading a prepared statement. He and Lucrecia had "some important issues to discuss" and wanted the time to do so alone. They were going out to dinner together and we could order pizza again. He also suggested that Laura and I use our time to think about how we'd acted today and reflect on the way we had decided to treat our guest, Lucrecia.

I was happy about the being-left-alone part, and the part about ordering pizza for the second night in a row. I wasn't as happy about being told to reflect on my actions, because I thought I had acted fine. It was an unnatural situation and I had reacted honestly. He wanted to know how I felt, and I told him. Just because it wasn't what he wanted to hear didn't mean I wasn't "behaving appropriately."

Laura was used to being told to go to her room and think about what she'd said or done. She shrugged it off and ordered our pizza as soon as Dad left. The board games were still strewn across the kitchen table, so we idly started a game of Scrabble as we waited for the delivery person.

"How does it feel to be the one in trouble?" Laura asked.

"You're in trouble too," I said.

"Not really," she said. "I was very polite to Lucrecia."

I laid the word "dumb" down on the Scrabble board. "What did you two talk about in the kayak?" I asked.

"Nothing, really. She said she wasn't going to ask me any questions, but she was an open book and I could ask her anything. I didn't really feel like asking her anything, but then she kept talking about how it's a shame to just keep looking at an open book without ever turning its pages and finding out what's inside. So I asked her about her divorce and she didn't want to talk about it."

"She didn't become an open book?"

"She said she could only tell her side of the story. And her side was that she had to leave the marriage. That's all she said. It seemed dark, so I didn't push it."

"Why not?" I said. "She wouldn't stop pushing me about Mom."

"What, exactly, did she say to you?" Laura asked.

"She said we don't 'explore our emotions.'"

"I explore my emotions," Laura said. She laid the word

"faulty" down on the Scrabble board. "Dad sent me to a therapist last year, you know."

"*What?* No. Are you serious?" I said.

"For like a month after school," she said. "When I was doing
all the cancer research."

"Why didn't you guys tell me?" I asked.

"I'm not a guy," she said. "I don't know. Dad said that he
thought I should talk to someone. And that you seemed okay."

"I mean, I would talk to someone too, if I had a good
option," I said. "Someone who isn't Lucrecia."

"You can talk to me," Laura said.

"I mean a professional," I said.

"I learned some things from the therapist."

"In your one month."

"I paid attention," she said.

"Well, how does it work?" I asked.

"We sit across from each other. Like we're already doing,"
she said. "Then I ask you something like, 'What would you like
to talk about today?'"

I waited for her to continue explaining how therapy worked.

"And then you answer . . ." she prompted.

"Oh, we're doing it?" I said.

"What would you like to talk about today?" she said with a
slight "adult" accent.

"My mother," I said.

"What about your mother?" she asked.

"She died two years ago," I said.

"And how does that make you feel?" she asked.

"Bad."

"Bad isn't an emotion."

"Sad."

"Are you sad all the time?"

"I mean, not all the time," I said. "Are *you* sad all the time?"

"I'm being the therapist here," she said.

"But you can also be my sister."

"Let's stay with me being the therapist," she said, returning to her adult voice. "Are you *always* sad?"

"No," I said. "It just . . . comes out of nowhere."

"Can you be more specific?"

"You know what I'm saying," I said. "I'll just be doing something and a memory of Mom will flash in my head. And even if it's a good memory, it only feels good for a second, and then I remember that she's gone, and there's nowhere for the memory to go. Dad doesn't want to talk about it, and you—" I stopped myself short.

Laura's face took on the expression she makes before she's about to cry. "You could share it with me," she said.

"But you always cry," I said.

Her adult voice started to slip. "Crying isn't a bad thing," she said.

"Are you saying this as the therapist or as yourself?"

"Both."

"Do you remember . . ." My eyes started to mist over.

"Tell me," Laura said, already fully crying.

"Do you remember the day we moved into the house?"

"And I knocked out my front tooth on the stairs," she said.

"And we all had to go to the emergency room."

"And Mom said it was a good omen to get our visit to the emergency room over on the first day and we'd spend the rest of the time in the house emergency-free."

We both smiled through our tears.

"Mrs. Stilden gave me a picture from that morning," I said. "It's in my backpack."

"Go get it," she said. "I want to see it."

As I went to get the photo from my backpack, the doorbell rang. Tears rolling down her cheeks, Laura pounced up with money in hand to answer the door. "Hi," she squeaked to the pizza delivery man.

"Whoa, hey," he said, looking from Laura to my own tear-streaked face as I returned to the kitchen. "Everything all right in there?"

"We're bonding," Laura said, taking the pizza.

"Have fun," he said confusedly.

# THIRTY-FIVE

**WHILE WE ATE,** we traded stories about Mom. It was the longest conversation we'd had since she died. For two hours, we reminisced without friction.

When I told Laura that I'd deleted all the pictures of Mom from my phone, she showed me a private album she kept at the bottom of her phone's photo stream. They weren't good pictures. She must have taken them when she was little, and they were kind of grainy, converted from an older phone, but they were enough.

The sky had darkened and we heard the unmistakable sound of a car parking outside. Then whispers and footsteps headed in two separate directions, those approaching the front door assumedly Dad's. We could have disguised what we were doing like we usually did. Laura could have swiped away all the pictures and pretended like we had just finished eating. But she didn't. We remained at the kitchen table, red-eyed from crying, the light streaks of tears still visible on Laura's cheeks. She left a picture of Mom's face on her phone's screen in the middle of the table, daring Dad to avoid it.

He opened the door cautiously and his eyes immediately fixed on the picture. He let out a deep breath. "Looking through some old . . ." he started, but stopped. "Can I see these?" he asked, sitting down and picking up the phone.

Laura and I both sat there watching him slowly scroll through the private album, waiting for what he'd say next. A single tear trickled down his left cheek. "Your mother was so beautiful," he said.

Laura jumped up and hugged him as he started to cry. I remained frozen in my chair, unsure whether I should join them or let them have their own private moment. Outside of his view, Laura waved for me to come over. I gingerly went over and hugged Dad on the left side.

For several seconds we hugged like a figurine of a loving family. Then Dad waved us off and motioned for us to sit back down in our own chairs. He wiped his tears away with his fingertips, took a deep breath in and out, and said, "I have a lot to say. And I want to get it all out."

"We have a lot to say too," Laura said.

"Can I just please go first?" he said quickly. "I'm sorry, I'm not angry. I just want to get this out right. And I want you to listen." He looked down at the table and inhaled to clear his sniffling nose. "Theo," he began, turning toward me. "I'm really sorry. Everything you said was right. Well, not everything. You said some things that I don't agree with. But, *mostly,* you were right. I went about this all wrong. Lucrecia and I were talking during dinner—"

"Can we not talk about her right now?" I said.

"It's connected, trust me," he said. "She's sorry too. She really is. She didn't mean to push you. But the real fault lies with me. I had a whole speech that I was going to give before we left for vacation and then I just got too nervous, and never gave it. And then I was going to say it later, but . . . I didn't. So I want to say it now. I have it written down. I hope that doesn't bother you. Just . . . give me a second."

He got up, went into the other room, and returned with a folded piece of graph paper.

This was the most serious I'd seen him since the day of the funeral. "No one will ever replace your mother," he started to read in a quavering voice. "Ever. She will always be your mother. The person who brought you into the world, raised you, and loved you."

I started sniffling as tears dribbled down my face. Next to me, Laura was full-on crying.

"It's okay," Dad said, as he reached to hold Laura's hand. "I don't want you to forget her," Dad continued. "And I'll never forget her. But we can also move on with our lives. We can't stay stuck in the past."

Laura got up to grab a small pack of tissues out of her backpack and returned holding a tissue to her nose. Wordlessly, she handed the pack over to me. I blew my nose as we waited to see if Dad had more to say.

He took a deep breath, folded the piece of graph paper back up, and tossed it on the table. "I never told you this, but your mom and I talked about what would happen to us, to our family, after she died. She said the only thing that mattered was our happiness. *Your* happiness. I don't know how happy you've been the last two years, but it's been a real rough time for me. I'm just starting to feel a little better, and Lucrecia has played a major part in that. She's not your mother, but right now she means a lot to me." He paused, motioned for the tissues, and delicately wiped at the corners of his eyes.

"Does that make sense?" he asked.

"Yes," we answered in unison.

# THIRTY-SIX

**DAD SAID HE WAS TIRED** of having emotional confrontations at kitchen tables, so we agreed to move outside to the back porch. The stars were so bright we didn't even need a light. Laura and I sat on a rocking bench while Dad leaned forward on a lounge chair.

"I wrote that a week ago," he explained. "But a lot has changed since then. Lucrecia and I already talked, but I want to hear your opinions. Your *real* opinions."

"Opinions about what, exactly?" I asked.

"About her," Dad said. "And me. The two of us together."

"Radical honesty?" Laura asked.

Dad lightly laughed. *"Radical honesty,"* he said.

"If I'm being one hundred percent honest, I . . . think . . . she's very nice," Laura said, *"but* I . . . would maybe have to get to know her better to under—"

"That doesn't sound one hundred percent honest," Dad said.

"Well, you just essentially said that you loved her, so, like, what am I supposed to say?" Laura said.

"Say what you feel," Dad said.

"You won't be mad?" Laura asked.

"I want to hear your real feelings," Dad said.

"Okay, well, I think she's a little much," Laura said.

"What do you mean *much?*"

"Like, she came in here and had this whole thing totally planned out. She took us to a spa and then the museum, and she paid for everything, and did everything she could to get on our good side. But then she wanted to, you know, coach us, and thought we'd just immediately love her for it," Laura said. "It was just *too much* for two days. Like, if she just acted like a normal person, I maybe would have liked her more. Not that she's a bad person, but you know what I mean."

I expected Dad to argue, to refute half of Laura's points, but he just said, "What else?"

"You were being all weird, too," I said. "Look at what you're wearing right now." He was wearing yoga pants and a tight black T-shirt.

"I like these," he said, looking down. "She bought these for me."

"Radical honesty?" Laura reminded him.

"I do feel a little silly in these pants," Dad said.

"And all that 'truly marvelous,' 'such a striking painting' stuff at the museum," I said.

"I can appreciate art," Dad said.

"You can, but you don't," I said.

"I try to," Dad said.

"Stop trying," I said. "It was embarrassing."

"And we saw you kiss," Laura said.

"What?" Dad nearly leaped out of his chair.

"At the museum," Laura said. "When we were up on that tower thing with the telescope that didn't work."

"I didn't think you could see from up there," Dad said. "I'm sorry. Seriously. I can't even—if I saw your grandma kissing someone, I don't know what I'd—"

"Ew, don't talk about Grandma kissing," Laura said.

"I'm trying to relate," Dad said.

"Do it in a less gross way," Laura said.

We all paused as a shooting star passed overhead. I made a wish that will remain secret.

"So what happens now?" Laura asked.

"What do *you* want to happen?" Dad asked.

"I want *you* to tell us what you and Lucrecia talked about," Laura said.

"Well"—Dad leaned back in his chair—"we both agreed that maybe we should take some time off."

"You're breaking up?" I asked.

"Not breaking up, exactly."

"Then what are you doing?" Laura asked.

"Taking a break."

"That sounds very similar," Laura said.

"She's leaving tomorrow morning and we'll see what happens from there," Dad said.

"Are you doing this because of us?" I asked.

"You don't want me to?" Dad asked.

"I mean, yes, I do," I said. "But I guess I just want to know why?"

Dad thought for a moment. "Because I don't think you two are ready. I moved a little too fast and forgot about *your* happiness. I wouldn't be honoring your mother if I didn't do what makes you two happy. Maybe in a couple months, we can get together again. We'll see how it goes."

He came over to join us on the rocking bench. We sat there gently swinging back and forth, watching the stars.

"You know I love you two, right?" Dad said.

"So you say," Laura said.

"Yeah, yeah," I said.

Dad laughed and pulled us both tight to his sides.

It'd been a long time since I'd seen him like this. I wish it hadn't required an eight-hour road trip, a birdwatcher and his dumb son, a bear attack, a nudist French couple, and his now somewhat-but-not-really ex-girlfriend to make him act more like his old self. But I would take it and enjoy it for as long as it lasted.

**I WOKE UP EARLY** the next morning. We'd stayed up late watching the stars, and Laura and Dad were still asleep. I wanted to be sleeping too, but the morning sun was shining directly into my eyes.

I took my notebook from my backpack and went out to the front porch. I flipped to where I had destroyed the drawings of Bob's favorite memories. Carefully, I removed the remaining bits of ripped paper and tried to make it look like nothing had happened.

On the last undamaged page, the scientist says he will demonstrate how the pill works. He hooks Bob up to a machine that projects all his memories onto a big screen. The scientist tells Bob to think of the happiest days of his life.

On a new page, I redrew Bob's fifth birthday party. His mom lifts a birthday cake up to his face as he blows out the candles. As I drew the extinguishing candles, the front door creaked open and Dad groggily stepped onto the porch, clutching a mug of coffee.

"You're up early," he said.

"The sun woke me up," I said.

"Looks like you're not the only one," Dad said, gesturing

toward Lucrecia's house. I hadn't looked earlier, but her car was already gone and the house was dark.

Dad sat down at the table next to me and took a sip of his coffee.

"I'm sorry," I said.

"Don't be sorry," he said. "Things will work out."

"I didn't *not* like her, you know," I said.

"We don't have to keep talking about it," he said. "What are you working on — your book?"

"Graphic novel," I said.

"Right, sorry," he said. "Graphic novel."

"I'm trying to. I kind of ripped out some pages, so I have to redo them."

"Why'd you rip them out? What happened on them?"

"You know what happened," I said. "Lucrecia told me you read it."

Dad looked down and whispered, "You caught me."

"Well, do you like it?" I asked hesitantly.

Dad scratched at his stubble. "I think . . . it's . . . wonderful," he said, breaking into a big smile.

I beamed back at him. "You're not just saying that?"

"I wouldn't lie to you."

"Yes, you would. And have. Very recently."

"I'm not lying about this." He took a long sip of coffee. "What did you rip up?"

"The part where Bob's remembering the best days of his life."

"I don't think I read that part," Dad said.

"Yeah, I just added it like three days ago."

"Can I see?" he asked.

I slid my notebook over to him. As he scanned the page, wrinkles formed in the corners of his eyes. "You know, she spent two months planning your fifth birthday party."

"Really?" I said.

"Really. It's hard work trying to book a real-life Sponge-Bob SquarePants. There aren't that many around Austin. And they're expensive. But she thought it was worth it. And she was right." He passed my notebook back to me. "What else does *Bob* remember?"

"I drew the time Mom picked me up early from school and took me to see *Mad Max: Fury Road*."

Dad laughed. "She hated that movie."

"No, she didn't," I said. "She said it was awesome."

"*You* said it was awesome. She said it was loud."

"Yeah, loud and awesome."

"She didn't want to criticize your favorite movie."

"It's not my *favorite* movie," I said.

"It was the day you saw it," Dad said. "How about the time you two raced up the down escalators at the mall?"

"And I beat her! But then the security guard came and yelled at us."

"I yelled at you a little bit too."

"I don't remember that," I said.

"Good," Dad said. He took another long sip of coffee. "What happens next?"

"What do you mean?"

"In the story. After Bob remembers all his favorite days, what happens?"

"Well," I said, "the scientist is trying to show him how the pill works. He wants to demonstrate how the pill will change his worst memories but also his best memories. He's doing, like, a simulation. So all of Bob's memories are on the screen in front of him, and then the scientist is going to press a button and it'll show Bob how a normal memory works."

"And then . . ." Dad prompted.

"The scientist presses the button and all the details from the best days of Bob's life slowly disappear. And he can only remember, like, little pieces."

"Why do they disappear?"

"Because that's what happens when you have a normal memory," I said. "Things keep fading away."

"Is that how you feel?" Dad asked.

"I . . . I just wish I could remember more."

He reached over and pulled me in for a hug. I settled my chin on the corner of his shoulder, wrapped my arms around him, and squeezed as hard as I could.

"I can help you remember," Dad said.

"You'd have to talk about her sometimes."

"I know," Dad said. "I will."

"And put the pictures back up," I said. "In the house."

"We'll see about that," Dad said.

"Just a few."

"You and Laura can pick some out."

"Do you promise?" I asked.

"I promise," he said. "So what does Bob decide? Does he take the pill?"

I paused for a moment to think. "No," I said. "He decides to remain Bob: The Boy with Perfect Memory."

# THIRTY-EIGHT

**WE MADE THE ENTIRE** return ride with only one stop. Because Dad didn't enforce his Family Road Trip Rules, Laura and I were able to sleep for most of it. When we pulled into our driveway at 10:00 p.m., I wasn't feeling very tired.

Dad was exhausted but wanted to fulfill his promise. After helping us dump all our things onto the living room floor, he fished out the flashlight from his backpack and made his way up to the attic.

He came down the stairs holding a long plastic container coated with a layer of dust. He set it down on the living room table before Laura and me like a sacred object.

"Who wants to do the honors?" he asked.

"Laura can do it," I said.

She popped the edges of the lid and coughed a little as dust flew into the air. Inside were six framed pictures, a few pieces of Mom's clothing, and a box of her jewelry. Laura took out each picture slowly and put them in a row in front of us.

Dad pointed to the picture of Mom holding baby Laura. "She thought you'd never stop crying. You cried your entire first week alive. This was the only picture we could find where you weren't sobbing."

"Not much has changed," I said.

Laura kicked me in the leg.

"Right after that one was taken," she said, pointing to a picture where we're all holding ice cream cones in front of Amy's Ice Creams, "you dropped your ice cream on the ground. Do you remember that?"

"No, I don't remember that because it didn't happen," I said.

"Yes, it did," she said.

"It did," Dad said.

He joined us on the couch as we took turns sharing our memories about each picture.

"How many can we keep out?" I asked.

"As many as you want," Dad said.

After they were all brought out in the open, we decided that none of the pictures could be banished back to the attic. Laura and I arranged them throughout the living room while Dad dragged our bags upstairs.

When he came back down, he sat between us on the couch.

"What do you think?" I asked.

His eyes slowly surveyed the redecorated room. "I think it's perfect," he said. He squeezed us in tight as we all looked at the pictures of Mom restored to their old place on the mantel.

I knew that this wouldn't last forever. That this could all recede and we'd fall back into our usual patterns in a few days. But for now, as the three of us huddled together on the living room couch, we felt like a truly happy family.

# ACKNOWLEDGMENTS

Thanks, first, to all my students who have inspired this book in numerous ways; to the fellow teachers who have helped me over the past decade, particularly Yvette Rocha-Held, David Fullen, Kia Jones, Abby DeShazo, A.J. Segoviano, and Natalie Anspaugh; to my friends Casey Prichard and Kevin Opp for inviting me on a trip that led to this story; to Sangeeta Mehta for her thoughtful, detailed feedback on the opening chapters; to Farahnaz Ghazizadeh and Lisa Goochee for their enthusiastic support of the first draft; to Jim McCarthy for taking a chance on me and guiding me through the entire publishing process; to Amy Cloud for making this book better and better with each edit; to Mary Claire Cruz for the wonderful cover art; to my family, particularly my sister Rachel and my aunt Wendy; and, most importantly, to Sanaz Talaifar, who has helped me in every aspect of my life and guided this book more than any other person.